Tales from a

Strange Southern Lady

Just look for the big pine right out there next to the highway * My name is Olivia * The position of caseworker was an unexpected addition to the many tasks I did while working at a local thrift store and charitable organization *

10 Short Stories

By Jan Fink

Fifth Estate, Post Office Box 116,

Blountsville, AL 35031

First Edition

Graphic Design by Will Fink

Printed on acid-free paper

Library of Congress Control No. 2014948396

ISBN: 9781936533473

Fifth Estate, 2014

This is for

Orenda and Christine

Contents

Life has been good, filled with the words and memories of many.
Their stories, road signs to the good, the funny and the bad
destinations in living life.

I.

C-R-A-Z-Y

"Just look for the big pine right out there next to the highway," Mama said and then in the same breath, "Oh, Anna honey, I'm sorry. I thought I wrote to you about the old man. He died about a year ago. Mr. Frank's in the Pines and I surely did think I had let you know about his passing. We put him next to the highway. You know how he liked to watch the cars pass. Remember how he'd sit for hours talking and staring through the screen door of that run-down old store of his, watching the cars pass on the highway? We thought he'd be happy with that plot in the Pines, bless his heart." Mama repeated "bless his heart," this time dragging out each word while gently tapping her chest, blessing her own heart in accordance with Mr. Frank's. Mama followed me out the front

9

door and down the walk, holding my sleeve, stopping along the way to pull weeds from her flower beds and still talking.

"I got some neighbors to go in with me. We pooled our money for the burial. Not much of a headstone but we did the best we could by the old man—even had it inscribed. Poor old soul, he was all alone in the world. Somebody had to do the Christian thing and bury him. That's exactly what I told the community. I said crazy as the old man was, we need to do the Christian thing." Mama's head nodded up and down in agreement with her own statement and again as I was leaving she shouted out, "The big pine, next to the highway, can't miss it."

Mama stood at the end of the walk, waving weed-filled fists in my rearview mirror. For two blocks the mirror held her image, growing smaller, still waving, the weeds in her fists going up and down like rough-cut pompoms. I turned onto the highway and the mirror replaced Mama with pavement and traffic.

Some things never change, Mama was Mama and she couldn't understand my unannounced arrival back home or my need to run off to a cemetery. I didn't explain. I could have said, "I came home to ask Mr. Frank a question. I need to know if I'm crazy. He would know and could tell me if I'm full blown, lost-in-the-head crazy. All his life people had said the old man was crazy, so he could tell me exactly how it felt. Mr. Frank may be dead and buried but I'm still going out to the cemetery to ask him my question." I could have said all that to Mama and it would have been the truth, but I didn't.

Five years earlier she had followed me down the same walk, pleading and gripping the suede of my coat hard enough to leave fingerprints.

"New York! New York City! Oh Anna, you just don't know the awful things that can happen to a young girl. Poppa and I told you we'd be glad to pay your tuition to trade school. Your sister Eva's going for her beautician license and plans to have her own shop someday. New York City, you alone in New York City! Anna, have you lost your mind?"

Mama then let go her grip on my sleeve, put one hand over her heart and the other to her forehead, saying if I went one step further down the walk she was going to faint. She didn't faint. Mama was standing right there at the end of the walk waving when I turned my car onto the highway.

Mama was right. I had lost my mind. Looking back, in all total I'd spent eight years in a state of temporary insanity. Back then she would've never been able to convince me of my mental state because I thought Mama was crazy. It happened overnight. One morning at age thirteen I woke up and Mama was crazy, and with the coming of each year I spent in adolescence Mama became more crazy. Insanity didn't just single out Mama. It included Poppa, my sister Eva, Miss Emma down the road, Mr. Frank at the grocery, my cousins and Preacher Ed, our minister. By the time I reached fifteen, the entire community had joined the ranks of crazy.

If you spent a little time in our neighborhood you'd agree with me. Mama had dreams that convinced her that she'd been a witch in her past life. To make up for it she spent all her time in church, doing the Christian thing as she called it. Poppa believed in Mama's dreams. He and Mama would be sitting in front of the TV watching Hulk Hogan pin someone to the mat and Mama would start babbling and pulling her hair. Poppa knew what to do. He'd run for the crucifix and chase Mama round the house till the past-life witch left her. Preacher Ed thought Mama was a good study. She became his mission in ministry. One summer he took her to the river and baptized her seven days in a row. Mama got all wrinkled up like a prune but kept having her dreams.

My sister Eva giggled her way through childhood and graduated to fainting in high school. Must say she did it well, just like in the movies, but after a while people tired of it and left her lying there where she'd swooned. My cousins were given rifles at the age of five and from then on they shot everything that posed a threat. Road signs, wild flowers, Mama's chickens — made no difference. They shot it.

And take Miss Emma. She spent the last ten years of her life sitting out on her front porch with her cats, willing her spirit into a camellia bush. Now Mr. Frank, well, everyone just said he was crazy, always had been. You can see what I was up against. Up to this point their effect on me had caused only a temporary insanity, but I considered myself a young woman who knew where she was going. I was going to the city where conversation was quick, educated, to the point. All you had to do was pick up any one of my sister Eva's magazines, read an article and you knew city people were different. Eva had a collection of movie magazines that were the pride and envy of everyone in town, but she never read the articles. She looked at the pictures and practiced in the mirror doing her makeup and hair like Faye Dunaway. I read the articles and I knew people in the city were different. They weren't crazy. I was going, never looking back, never coming back.

There were other explanations I couldn't give Mama. I couldn't explain the awful things that can happen to a young girl. During the years spent in New York I was mugged by a pair of young men with caution-light yellow hair for the sum total of two dollars and seventy-nine cents; my car was towed more times than I can count; I met people so educated that they had no more common sense than a well-bred dog; my apartment was burglarized—they took everything but the orange crate bookshelves, and every day there were crowded subway rides where hands roamed and old men leered.

People in the city were different. They were crazy too. Mean crazy. Work was hard to find. I drifted from one job to another; then a waitress at a café down on West Thirty-fourth Street where I often stopped in said she could get me on waiting tables if I didn't mind the work. I didn't mind but after three weeks I still couldn't remember the restaurant language. They'd yell "B.L.T. and make it Seaboard" and I'd just stand there not knowing what to do. Then one day a customer said, "You've got a funny accent. Where are you from?" I told him Alabama. He laughed and said, "I bet you could call some hogs for me." That was the straw that broke me.

They say I threw back my head, yelled "Sooooiee!" and then ran from the café crying, wearing my apron and still holding my order pad and pencil, but I don't remember. I don't remember being found on the sidewalk out front of the Paper Moon Emporium in white greasepaint, a hand full of paper sunflowers, walking an imaginary tightrope and asking where the movie magazine article people were. That's what they told me when I woke up to find a woman in the bed next to mine, holding a doorknob in her hand and trying to diaper it with a piece of tissue. Bellevue kept me for two weeks. I told them insanity runs in my family. I told them I came from an entire community of crazies. They wanted to know if there was anyone they should call, but I said no, I knew the way home.

So here I was back and nothing changes, but it had changed. Mr. Frank was gone. I felt cheated. Everything had changed. When I reached Miss Emma's house, I slowed the car. Vinyl siding had been installed. The camellia bush next to the porch was in full bloom, but there were no cats in the yard. A sign over the latticed porch read:

"Curl up and Dye"

Y'all Stop In

Eva Strickland, Owner

I didn't stop in. I was sure Mama had been on the phone the minute I was out of sight, letting Eva know I was back in town and how unexpected it all was, but Eva could wait. Preacher Ed's house was different, not so much the house but in the yard there were six scruffy children, three junk cars and an old washing machine turned on its side. It was Preacher Ed's house, but I felt he didn't live there anymore. Mr. Frank's Grocery had a fresh coat of paint and a new sign that spelled out his name in neon and offered cold beer. Mr. Frank wouldn't have liked that but it didn't matter. The old man wasn't there anymore; he was in the Pines.

It was late afternoon when I reached the Pines Cemetery. Clouds carrying a fine mist rain had rolled in from the east, blocking the sun, darkening the sky. The Pines covered less than a two-acre square of fine sandy earth wedged in between the highway on the front and fresh-plowed fields to the rear and along both sides. A rutted dirt and gravel road made a half-moon path around the cemetery then back out to the highway. There was no sign, just lines of plain headstones and leaning plot markers anchored only by the powdered sand. Arrangements of plastic mums, Shasta daisies, tulips and roses, their color bleached by the sun, lay like centerpieces upon each plot. Long leaf pines grew throughout the cemetery, shading and standing guard over those resting beneath their limbs. They ranged in size from head-high saplings to towering, cloud touching giants.

I reached Cousin Jimmy's grave first. I must have been ten and Jimmy was just starting out in life when he and a quart of Jack Daniels met a busload of kids out on Highway 43 coming home from a homecoming game. None of the kids on the bus were hurt, but Jimmy didn't make graduation that year. I remember his mama, Aunt Cathy, had an arrangement made in the shape of the diploma he never got and placed it on his plot that day when he was brought to the Pines. Miss Emma was just a few rows down from Jimmy and next to her was Preacher Ed. I guess that's another letter Mama thought she wrote.

Further down next to the highway stood the largest pine and Mr. Frank's resting place. Mama and the neighbors had done well by the old man. His grave site beneath the tall pine was outlined with small white stones and there were no artificial arrangements. The old man would have been grateful for their absence. The headstone was small and plain, the inscription simply,

Mr. Frank

? – 2012

With Jesus Now

I sat down, my back against the rough bark of the pine. Looking across the cemetery I thought of how far I'd run, how I had distanced myself. Through the distance, as if by a contrived conspiracy, the old man and the others had up and left. I was back home but they weren't coming back; they had run the final distance. I still had my question. I asked the empty cemetery, "How does crazy feel?"

The needles of the big pine watching over Mr. Frank caught the rain, now graduated from mist to slow, rhythmic drops. The air smelled of wet pine, rain-peppered soil and steamy plastic roses, their petals sweltering and gummy, sun-hot and moist from the rain. From the fresh plowed field behind me a child laughed.

# # #

It was Eva's laughter. I braced myself for the punch in the ribs that always followed Eva's sudden outburst of uncontrollable giggles.

"He's gonna do it again; he's gonna talk to Jesus." Eva's shrill voice filled the cemetery. Mama took Eva by the arm, pulled her out of the rain, back under the umbrella and swatted her behind so hard it lifted her up off the ground, her patent leather shoes spraying mud droplets. It did little good; Eva giggled on. Mama trying to correct her rude spells was useless.

We were laying Miss Emma to rest that day. The pines, not long planted, stood only a few feet high and did nothing to block out the rain, falling steady since noon. Preacher Ed had said his last words over Miss Emma; she'd been covered and Mama was saying what a shame it was, rain and all on the day of Miss Emma's taking to the ground. The neighbors had made arrangements of artificial flowers shaped in hearts, crosses, the face of Jesus and cats, for which Miss Emma had a great fondness. They were placed on top of the fresh earth like well wishes. Mama commented that she wished Miss Emma could be there to see what a fine turnout it was and wouldn't the sight of those arrangements just take Miss Emma's breath away. Eva was still laughing out of control, but it wasn't Mama causing her rude spell. Mr. Frank had made his way through the crowd of mourners and standing right there over Miss Emma's arrangement of Jesus' face he raised his hands to the sky.

"Sweet Jesus, don't ever give me nothing that last forever. Now you take those plastic flowers," he said, pointing toward the Jesus face of mums and roses, "They never need any water but go on forever. If Jesus meant us to have flowers like this he would have put them here in the beginning. Not natural I tell you, plain not natural." Eva lost all control, punched me in the ribs, fell to the ground and rolled in the mud while Mama hollered about Eva ruining her good Sunday dress.

The rain stopped long enough that afternoon for Mama to let me and Eva walk down to Mr. Frank's Grocery. Mama said she was letting Eva go to the store because the walk would do her good and she wanted Eva to do some thinking. Thinking about how she had behaved being so awful and rude at the funeral. I think Mama just wanted some peace and quiet. Eva skipped along, jingling the change in her pocket and talked rather than thinking.

"They're all crazy, you know," Eva said, screwing her face up, doing her "I'm nuts" imitation.

"Who?"

"Mama, Mr. Frank, Miss Emma, the whole bunch. Every one of them got rooms to rent upstairs."

"Eva, you shouldn't talk like that."

"Why not? Preacher Ed's always saying the truth will set you free and I'm talking truth and I am free." Eva went into double skips, running ahead then turning back. She said, "I got an idea. You know how Miss Emma said she was never gonna die, how she'd live forever in that big camellia bush out there next to her porch? I say we go over there and ask her how she's feeling."

"Eva, Miss Emma is in the Pines and you know it."

"I know it but does Miss Emma know she's in the Pines? While we're standing here talking Miss Emma could be over there in that bush waiting for someone to drop in and say hello."

It never did any good to argue with Eva. She was going to do exactly as she pleased. When we reached Miss Emma's house Eva skipped right up to the camellia bush, gave a slight curtsy, holding the hem of her dress at arm's length and in a honey sweet voice said, "Good evening Miss Emma, we just wanted to stop by and see how you're feeling."

One of Miss Emma's cats answered for her. The half wild calico Miss Emma called Patches ran screeching and spitting from beneath the bush. It went straight through Eva's legs, made a crazy quilt path through the yard and took off down the highway. Still holding the hem of her dress, Eva was jumping from one foot to the other screaming and giggling. I was certain my heart had stopped, but nothing bothered Eva. She punched me in the ribs again and between her giggles she gasped, "Oh Anna, I do believe I've wet my pants." She turned back to the bush and talking honey sweet again said, "Nice talking with you Miss Emma" and was off skipping toward Mr. Frank's Grocery.

# # #

A semi loaded with crates of chickens passed on the highway. The driver sounded his horn and waved to me. The chickens, wet from the rain, bounced along behind him, white with staring, frightened red eyes. I leaned forward, waved then settled back against the pine, my clothing wet and plastered to my back. I was as soaked as the passing chickens but I couldn't bring myself to leave the cemetery, the pines, memories and the old man.

# # #

Mr. Frank was out front working on his sign when Eva and I reached his store. With a black permanent magic marker in his scrawling penmanship he was adding the words "and Greens" next to Minnows, Fishing Worms, Cold Sodas." He stood back and looked over his work smiling, proud of his sign. Eva closed one eye and stuck her thumb out looking from one side of it to the other like she'd seen artists do on TV.

"That looks pretty good, Mr. Frank. But why don't you get yourself a new sign, one of those pretty neons like they have in town?"

"Little Eva, I don't want nothing to do with neon. Neon makes me terrible nervous. One day while I was driving through town I ran all the way off the road being distracted by one of them flash-flashing neons. You girls mark my word, within five years them flashing neon signs will spread across the South like boll weevils. And I'll tell you something else; they'll be folks running off the road and having wrecks because of them. Now what good could come from that? No good at all cause folks will be having wrecks and getting killed, all because of them neons."

"Did Jesus tell you that?"

I could have slapped Eva for the question but the old man didn't seem to mind. He reached out, patted Eva's head and said, "There are some things Jesus don't have to tell you. You just figure it out all by yourself." Eva pretended to understand, then with a roll of her eyes she motioned me toward the screen door of the store. I followed a few steps behind her and Mr. Frank called out.

"Anna?"

"Yes sir."

"You don't talk much. Guess your sister Eva there does most of the talking for you. Your eyes have the shine you know. They shine like those flat rocks you skip along the top of water. You talk with your eyes, Anna."

I said "Yes sir," then hurried on behind Eva into the dim yellow light of the old store. Eva pulled two RC Colas from the cooler, handed me one and rolled her eyes again. "Told you he was crazy."

Everyone in the neighborhood considered Mr. Frank to be crazy. None of them ever gave a concrete reason, just went around whispering about how odd he was. His grocery had been there forever. No one knew exactly how old he was. With the exception of a slight graying of the stubble that cloaked his face the old man didn't change much throughout the years. He dressed in duplicates of the same beige work pants, flannel shirts of red and green plaid and a small felt hat pulled low over his brow. In summer when watermelons were in season he brought them from his garden and with his black magic marker he wrote on each side of the melons: "Blessed are the poor in spirit for theirs is the kingdom of Heaven;" "Suffer the little children to come unto me;" and Jesus wept." Then he'd line the melons up end to end along the highway frontage of his store. On the grass next to the melons he'd stick up a small plywood sign which read:

Watermelons 50 cents

Scripture Free

One summer night some of my cousins drove by the grocery and shot up all of Mr. Frank's melons. Next morning the old man cleaned up the mess, went to his garden, brought back more melons and started over. He said Jesus talked to him and that he was bound by Jesus to share their conversations. Jesus had told Mr. Frank to put those scripture melons along the highway and no matter how many times they were shot up he'd replace them. The boys finally gave up, stopped coming in the night. It was no fun when the old man wouldn't get mad.

# # #

"How upset you were, Cousin Jimmy. All that wasted ammo and not one cross word from Mr. Frank." My voice sounded hollow and lost across the empty cemetery. There was no response. I picked up a pebble and tossed it toward Jimmy's grave. Thunder rolled across the cemetery. The rain storm was now considerable and threatening. I held my position under the pine. The sky was crying, crying for me. I wanted more than anything to reach through the sandy earth, down deep into the ground and pull the old man out of his coffin. With one finger I probed the wet sand, gauging the possibility of digging and dragging Mr. Frank out, then propping him up against the tall pine next to me. Or better yet, I could take him down the road, back to his grocery and sit him out front on his favorite old pine stump. Then we could talk. I would buy a cola and sit next to him like Eva and I did years ago. Then I'd ask him. I'd say, "Mr. Frank, how does crazy feel?"

# # #

Eva and I brought our colas outside. Watermelons were in season and Mr. Frank was sitting out next to the road on an old pine stump with a watermelon in his lap, busy writing on its slick green belly. Eva ran to him and peered over his shoulder.

"Mr. Frank, how long has Jesus been talking to you?"

"A long, long time child." The purr of a car's engine came swiftly from the south. Mr. Frank stopped writing, looked over his shoulder, watching till the car came into view then followed its progress till it was out of sight before he turned back to Eva.

"Jesus didn't talk to me when I was a young man. I was a drunkard, a gambler, abused my family. Lost my family but even that didn't get my attention. Then one night I was out there in my garden trying to find my way back to the store. I was drunk as a chicken, stumbling and falling every two to three feet when I heard a voice behind me. I turned to see who it was and I found the devil standing there." Eva gave out a half-hearted giggle, but I could tell the old man had her attention.

"The devil was smiling at me with his arms out stretched." The old man leaned forward and extended his arms, a grin thinning the stubble on his chin. "Looked just like this." Eva took a step back, her eyes wide.

"Sure as I'm sitting here girls, that devil had come to claim me." Mr. Frank looked back down at the melon in his lap and began to write. Eva couldn't control herself.

"So what did you do?"

"I'll get to that but first I've got to tell you that when I looked real close at the devil, he was me. Had my face but it was red and twisted and grinning and the mouth on it was saying, "Come on Frank, you know it's time." Mr. Frank paused. Eva impatiently stamped her foot and demanded again.

"What did you do?"

"I turned my back on that me-devil and when I looked ahead there was Jesus. That's when I knew I had a choice and I chose Jesus. Jesus has talked to me ever since that night." Eva let out a grunt.

"Well, seems to me if somebody really saw the devil their hair would turn white and they'd go running and screaming. You ready to go Anna?"

"That may be so," Mr. Frank said, and smiled. "Come to recollect, I did do some running and screaming that night, but it was because Jesus saved me from that me-devil. Here, this is for you Eva. On the house." The old man handed her the melon he'd been working on. "And tell your mama I have fresh greens." Eva took the melon. On it was written "Do unto others as you would have them do unto you." We walked back down the highway, Eva complaining and shifting the weight of the melon from one hip to the other.

"Me-devil? He was the devil. What did I tell you Anna? C-R-A-Z-Y. That's how you spell Mr. Frank."

# # #

The laughing child from the field ran barefoot into the cemetery, jumping graves, landing in puddles till she reached me. "What's your name?" she asked.

"Anna."

She looked down at the old man's headstone. "You know him?"

"Yes. I used to visit his store."

She looked at the headstone again. "My mother said he was crazy." Then she laughed and bugged out her eyes. She looked so much like Eva. Precocious little Eva who was now all grown up, at this moment down the road in Miss Emma's house doing hair and nails just like in the movie magazines. I felt the tears begin. They fell onto my cheeks and were lost in the rain.

"C-R-A-Z-Y. That's how you spell Mr. Frank." The words spilled out, my voice choked with the lost tears. The little girl looked at me.

"He once told me my eyes had the shine. He said I talked with my eyes. He met the devil in his garden late one night. Jesus talked to him. Told him to write scripture on watermelons. Mr. Frank was crazy. Good crazy."

The little girl kneeled and moved her fingers along the inscription on the headstone as she read it out loud. "His stone says he's with Jesus now."

"Yes, he is. I imagine he and Jesus are having some grand conversations."

The rain still fell; a gust of wind picked up the remains of a discarded plastic rose. It bobbed along the sand; its petals danced in a tiny whirlwind across Jimmy, Miss Emma and Preacher Ed then landed inside the white stone outline under Mr. Frank's pine. I picked it up and tossed it to the highway. A car sped by, scattering the rose, carrying loose petals further down the pavement. The little girl watched me, her eyes bright and curious.

I thought I heard the old man say, "You just figure it out all by yourself," but wind in a cemetery has a way of its own. Talks to you sometimes.

"You live here?" the girl asked.

"Yes. I've always lived here."

"Never seen you around."

"I've been lost for a while."

"You want to play?" She waited for my answer, restlessly moving her toes along the sandy earth, making little creek beds for the rain to fill.

"No. Not today. I think I'm going to stop in, maybe see my sister Eva, Mama, Poppa and all the cousins."

II.

Dancing with the Redbirds

My name is Olivia. It was two days past my ninth birthday that Poppa told us we were moving. He told me to take Little Charlie's wagon to the corner store and bring back boxes for packing.

I did as Poppa said, then took Little Charlie to our room to pack our things. When I was finished Poppa said I did a good job. He didn't know I had to pack most of the boxes twice because Little Charlie kept unpacking them. He didn't want a new home. Over the years we had moved a lot but that didn't bother me. It was different with Little Charlie. We had lived in this home since he was born.

We left early the next morning. The day was beautiful, full of sun and blue skies. Little Charlie and I rode in the back seat on top of boxes filled with Mama's pots and pans. Poppa was so happy. As he drove he sang the funniest songs he knew. Each time Mama tried to ask him a question about our new home he sang louder.

When we reached the house Poppa jumped from the car, held up his arms like a magician and sang out "Taa Daa!" Then he bowed as if he had made the house appear out of thin air. Mama let out a gasp and I knew why. It was the biggest house I'd ever seen. There were three stories with porches and balconies and pointed towers that seemed to reach right up to the clouds. I had seen castles in story books and this was a castle.

"Oh, Poppa! Are we really going to live in this castle?"

"Olivia, this is not a castle. It's just a house, our new home."

What Poppa said made no difference to me. It was a castle and I'd always call it our castle. Poppa hurried us onto the porch, slipped the key in the lock and pushed open the door. Once inside Mama stood in the entrance hall holding Little Charlie's hand. She looked tired and worried as she turned to Poppa.

"We can't afford this."

"Sure we can, Mama. I got it for a song."

Everyone laughed except Mama. What Poppa said was funny because that's just what Poppa did for a living. He was a singer of songs. He sang anywhere for anyone if they paid him. Mama once told me that Poppa stood in the shallows of a river and sang for a baptism during one of the worst thunderstorms to ever hit south Alabama. He'd been wearing the only dress suit he owned and it shrank up small enough to fit a child. Mama said that what he got paid for his singing that day wasn't even enough to replace his suit much less put food on the table. She told me that standing in a river in a dress suit singing during a thunderstorm didn't make sense to her but that Poppa always did as he pleased no matter what she thought. I could see that same look on her face now, like the day she told me that story.

Little Charlie broke free of Mama's hand and ran the length of the hall to the stairway. He climbed the stairs with his short little legs till he reached the middle step. He stood on the step, holding to the banister and forcing his weight up and down, making the step creak.

"Mama, Livia says this is a castle. We gonna live in this castle?"

"Your Poppa says we are."

"Indeed we are. Happily ever after." Poppa began to hum, putting his arm around Mama, taking her for a tour of the downstairs. Little Charlie and I did our own exploring. We ran from room to room and floor to floor. Some rooms were big enough to play ball in and others as small as closets. The house seemed to never end. We discovered a secret passage between two of the second story bedrooms. I asked Poppa if Little Charlie and I could have those rooms. Poppa said the passage was meant to store wood for the bedroom fireplaces during the winter but we could have the rooms and use the secret passage to come and go between our bedrooms during the summer.

Little Charlie was glad to have the secret passage. He had bad dreams and with the passage he could come into my room, sleep with me and feel safe. He made me promise that when winter came I would make a path amid the wood so he could always use the passage. I told him not to worry — that winter was a long time away. He began to cry.

"Livia, I don't ever want winter to come. I hate this castle. I wanna to go home!"

I held him and promised once again to make a path in our secret passage no matter how much wood Poppa piled in there. He stopped crying and seemed satisfied but only for a short time. During our first weeks in the castle the slightest cool summer breeze would send Little Charlie running upstairs crying and checking the secret passage.

Mama didn't like the castle either. One night during dinner she told Poppa the castle had thirteen rooms. Poppa teased her saying she was superstitious. Mama told him to keep quiet, that she had counted each and every one of the rooms and it came to thirteen and thirteen was bad, unlucky. She told Poppa she wanted to find another house but Poppa didn't answer her, just shook his head no and finished his dinner in silence.

After dinner Little Charlie and I went up to our secret passage. We sat in the tiny space playing ball and jacks and talked. Little Charlie thought Mama believed the castle was bad because winter was coming. He didn't want winter to come either because he would be so cold. He said he'd had a dream and Mama was right. When winter came the castle would be bad because it had thirteen rooms. I told him to stop worrying about winter and that the castle having thirteen rooms didn't mean anything. He looked up at me; his little face filled with sadness and he said, "It does, Livia. Thirteen rooms mean something. Something bad."

There were only two houses on our street. The castle and next door a small cottage where an older lady called Miss Adele lived. She came over to welcome us with a plate of oatmeal raisin cookies and a pitcher of fresh lemonade. We sat in the kitchen eating the cookies while she and Mama got to know each other. Mama asked her if she knew the history of the castle and Miss Adele gave out a short laugh and rolled her eyes.

"Oh honey, this old place got more history than me and you will ever have in a lifetime. It was built in the early 1800s as a wedding present. My lot and little house was once a part of this estate. I know the history of just about every piece of property in this town. You see when I first moved here I joined the Historical Society. I was young and had a great need to know everything back then. I learned a lot, maybe more than I wanted to. I don't belong to the Historical Society anymore. Now days I refer to that organization as the Hysterical Society. At one time it was a good thing but over the years the meetings became nothing more than a reason for a bunch of old hens to get together and have garden parties and share gossip."

"So you do know the history of our house, Miss Adele?"

"Sorry, dear, I tend to rattle in my old age. Yes, I know all about your house. You know that big stretch of property across the street, well, there used to be an even bigger Victorian monstrosity over there than what you got here. It burned about twenty-five years ago. Surprised it didn't long before that. The roof had caved in and it had stood abandoned for years. It was full of rats and got to be a party place for the young hoodlums in town. If you were to ask one of the Hysterical Society members today about the history of that house they wouldn't be able to tell you a thing about it. Not that they don't know the history, but because they consider it bad history.

"Anyway, that long gone Victorian and your house were built by Judge Fox. Your house like I said was built as a wedding present for his only surviving child, Nathan. The judge's wife had six stillbirths before she died giving birth to Nathan. The judge never remarried and I imagine he had his hands full raising his son alone. Court records show Nathan spent most of his life in one kind of trouble or another. Fact is he shot and killed a man right out there in the street for spitting in front of his wife. Any other man would have hanged for it but old Judge Fox had connections and he pretty much had the whole town in his pocket. Nathan never spent so much as an hour in jail no matter what his crime.

"The judge was so pleased when Nathan decided to marry. He liked the young girl and over the years she was an anchor to Nathan, keeping him out of trouble. But she was a frail little thing and within the first ten years of their marriage she had eight stillborn babies and died trying to deliver the last one. When she died Nathan took to the drink and one early winter morning the judge came over here and found him hanging up there from the third floor banister. Right above where we're sitting right now."

Miss Adele pointed above her head. Little Charlie had been focused on the plate of cookies up to this point. He looked up, dropped the half eaten cookie in his hand and ran to Mama.

"Mama, dead people lived in our house? I wanna go home! I wanna go home, Mama!"

"Oh dear, I am sorry. I didn't think the child was even listening to me go on. Don't cry, child. Miss Adele just telling your Mama some old stories, that's all it is, old stories."

"That's okay, Miss Adele. He's probably tired and had too many sweets today. Olivia, take Charlie upstairs. I think he could use a nap."

I took Little Charlie up to his room and he fell asleep quickly. I went back downstairs and stood in the dining room next to the kitchen out of sight so I could hear more of the history of the castle. Miss Adele was still apologizing for upsetting Little Charlie.

"I don't know what I was thinking, dragging up such a book of sadness and upsetting your sweet child that a way. I best be getting home. You probably don't want to hear one more word out of my loose mouth."

"No, please stay Miss Adele. I do want to know everything about this house. To tell you the truth I don't really like this house. I'm not sure why. It has thirteen rooms, you know. My husband laughs at me and calls me superstitious when I mention it, but why would anyone build a home with thirteen rooms? It seems to me they were tempting fate. Moving here was all my husbands' idea. I had never laid eyes on the place till he packed us up and dropped us at the front door. If I'd seen it beforehand I would have put my foot down and stayed put in the nice little home we had. So please—stay and tell me all you know of this place."

"Well okay. There's not much more to the story. After his son hung himself Judge Fox sat over there across the street in his house. The view of this house from his front windows was a constant reminder of the loss of his son. It's said he died of heart break with no heirs or relatives to claim either property. So his house sat neglected and falling in till it burned. This house of yours sat neglected too till the late forties, when it was sold at auction to a young couple from out of town. Word is they sunk a lot of money toward fixing this old place up but you wouldn't think that now. You and your husband got your work cut out for you making this place livable. Yes in all, this house has changed owners more than two dozen times over the years. Nobody stayed here long and no matter how much they invested in it, the old house seemed to have a mind of its own. Kinda like a death wish if such a thing is possible with an inanimate object."

"I'm not sure what you mean, Miss Adele."

"I mean that no matter how much the owners tried to reclaim the beauty of this old house, the house fought back. I mean the house wanted to die, be gone like its creator Judge Fox and all who had lived in it. You know the Judge, his wife, son, daughter-in-law and all those stillborn babies are buried in the cemetery at the end of this street. If it was possible I believe this house would like to be right there with them. Gone and buried."

"I'm sorry Miss Adele, but I have to admit you're scaring me now."

"Oh, fiddle. Don't pay a smidge to what comes out of my mouth. I'm just a rambling old woman who likes a good story. Truth be known the reason this house had so many owners is because the place is impossible to heat, cool or keep up. That's all there is to it. Don't let a word I've said scare or worry you in the least little bit. I'm glad to have neighbors and here I go scaring them off with this mouth of mine. You make yourself a nice home here and let me know if there is anything at all I can help with. I've out-stayed my welcome. Tell those children of yours Miss Adele will be back with more sweet treats in a few days. Goodbye and God bless."

I joined Mama in the kitchen. She stood at the window watching Miss Adele cross the yard. "Olivia, did you hear the rest of Miss Adele's story?"

"Yes, Mama."

"Don't get me wrong Olivia. She's a dear old lady but I think she stretches the truth a bit. You shouldn't be upset by any of the things she said about this house. Probably old tales she's heard over the years with little to no truth to them."

"I'm not upset Mama. I like this castle and hearing the stories she told us."

"Good. I got to tell you she had me going there for a moment. And there I was talking about thirteen rooms tempting fate and spurring her on. Your Poppa was right. When we first came here I got caught up in superstitious nonsense. Poppa will be home from his singing engagement day after tomorrow, so why don't we surprise him and clean this place from top to bottom."

We took broom, mop, bucket, polishes and wax and started on the first floor. Mama and I worked side by side cleaning the first floor then working our way up to the third floor landing. I stood looking at the banister and ran my hand along the smooth wood.

"Mama, this is where Miss Adele said the Judge's son hung himself. Why do you think he'd pick such a place?"

"Put it out of you mind Olivia. Just a story, an old story with no truth to it. This is our home, or as you say our castle, and we're going to make it shine. Get busy—we have a lot to do before Poppa gets home."

When all thirteen rooms were done the castle smelled of lemon oil. Little Charlie walked around holding his nose saying "That stinks. This castle stinks. I wanna go home."

"You are home, Charlie. Now uncover that cute little nose so I can give it a kiss." Little Charlie let go of his nose long enough for Mama to give him a kiss then promptly covered it again.

Poppa arrived home and was amazed at how beautiful Mama and I had made the castle.

"I am so proud of you ladies that from now on each time I come home from a singing engagement I'm going to bring a what-not, vase or a piece of furniture till we fill up every room in this house."

Throughout the summer Poppa brought home odds and ends from junk stores and yard sales and we found just the right place for them in each room. On one of our explorations on the property Little Charlie and I discovered a rock garden and next to it a stone bench and table. It was all covered with vines and choked with weeds but when we called Mama out to see our find she said it was a wonderful treasure. It took two days to clear away all the vines and weeds, then we washed down the bench and table. Mama planted flowering cactus and ferns in the rock garden, making it beautiful and inviting.

It became our special place and we spent the good days of summer at the stone table eating fresh cucumber sandwiches and cold tomato soup in the bright summer light.

Poppa made bird feeders from old coffee cans that Mama painted with scenes of blue skies and round smiling sun faces. We hung them in the rock garden and soon a family of Cardinals began to come and feed daily. They'd eat and skitter along the back of the stone bench, then jump to the ground hopping around before taking flight. Little Charlie called them Redbirds. When I corrected him telling him they were Cardinals, Mama said, "Olivia if Little Charlie says they're Redbirds, then Redbirds they will be."

When the Redbirds came during our picnics Mama would point at them and say, "Look Little Charlie! Would you just look at the Redbirds dance?" Little Charlie would tuck his arms to his chest and flap his elbows like wings and dance with the Redbirds. He was so happy, his nightmares gone, the fear of the coming winter forgotten.

He was happy till the days of summer grew shorter. When the leaves began to fade and drop from the trees and the air grew cooler Mama stopped our picnics in the rock garden. Little Charlie fell silent and moody as he watched Poppa cut wood and store it away in the cellar and our secret passage. When Poppa was finished our passage was filled wall to wall to ceiling. Little Charlie tugged at my sleeve with tears filling his eyes.

"Member Livia? Member your promise?"

I took the wood stick by stick and hid it under my bed till I had cleared a path just as I had promised. When winter's cold air settled in Poppa kept the fireplaces in our bedrooms burning all day and long into the night. He complained about the missing wood and brought up more from the cellar filling the passage again. When the space beneath my bed could hold no more wood I carried it to the cellar, keeping the path clear for Little Charlie.

Even in this effort to console him he had become unusually quiet. He began wearing his winter jacket constantly, even as he slept with the jacket hood pulled tight about his face. He lost interest in games or stories and sat quietly, his pale face framed by the hood. It was as if something had come in and replaced his eyes, stolen them in the night and leaving him with a look of strangeness. The eyes that stared out of the jacket hood were those of an old man who had seen too much and knew too much. His nightmares were back. I would hear him in the night crying out and squeeze through the passage and carry him back to my bed. He would stop crying and when I woke in the morning he would be gone, back in his own bed.

The winter nights became bitter. No matter how much wood Poppa carried in or how hot a fire he built the cold stayed with us. The constant winds blew through the walls and windows of the castle so visible you could reach out your hand and touch it. Little Charlie took to his bed, refusing to get up. I tried to get him to play his favorite game of ball and jacks but he shook his head no and pulled the covers tighter around his shoulders.

"I'm too cold. I told you when winter came the castle would be bad. Thirteen rooms like Mama said. Thirteen rooms are bad. The babies told me the castle was bad too. They said I should go home."

"What babies?"

"The dead born babies in my room. They're cold too."

"Are you talking about that story Miss Adele told us? Mama said that was nothing but a story and there's no truth to it. Little Charlie, there are no dead babies in this house."

"The babies are here! You just shut up, Livia. The dead born babies want you to shut up too. We're all cold and we want you to shut up!"

I went downstairs and told Mama what he'd said about the dead born babies in his room. Mama stared past me, her face distant as if she weren't hearing me.

"Could be fever. He's been pale lately. Come help me Olivia."

Mama made a tray with sandwiches and a glass of milk, then went to the hall wardrobe and took out all the quilts inside, draping them over her arm. "Come upstairs with me and bring the tray." At the door to Little Charlie's room Mama told me to wait with the tray. She went to his bedside and covered him with all the quilts then came and took the tray from me. She carried it to his bedside table. I leaned in the doorway, "Little Charlie, are the babies here now?" Little Charlie didn't move or look in my direction.

Mama told me to go back downstairs and I lingered in the hall trying to listen. I could hear them speaking in low tones. Mama stayed in his room all afternoon and was still there when I went to my room at bedtime.

Mama didn't come downstairs till noon the next day. She looked as if she hadn't slept at all. She took two boxes of Pop Tarts from the cabinet and a quart of milk from the fridge, made a tray and went back upstairs to Little Charlie's room. I wandered about the house, bored and missing my brother. Poppa wasn't due home for another two weeks. Lately he'd taken a lot of singing jobs and was away from home most of the time. Two weeks was so far away. I was frightened and needed him home now.

For the next week Mama continued to take meals up to Little Charlie's room. I ask if I could visit him but she said no. Up till a week ago Mama had been bringing wood from the cellar and keeping the fireplaces burning throughout the house, but now one by one the fires burned out and Mama didn't rebuild them. The castle became unbearably cold. I managed to build a fire in my room using lots of paper to start the wood. Other than going to the kitchen for Pop Tarts or a sandwich I spent my time in my room near the fire.

By the end of the second week Mama locked the door to Little Charlie's room and carried the key with her when she was not there with him. She nailed shut the entrance to the secret passage in his room. Late at night I'd go into the passage and sit next to the door and call out to him but he never answered. I'd sit and read aloud the stories he enjoyed and play a game of ball and jacks, me taking his turn and letting him win but there was only silence from the other side of the door. Each time Mama came downstairs she looked more terrible than the day before and she rarely spoke. I ask if she was sick and maybe I should go get Miss Adele.

"Olivia, have you seen the babies?"

"No, Mama."

"If you do you'll tell me won't you?"

"Yes, Mama."

I was telling the truth; I hadn't seen the babies. I didn't believe there were any babies. Mama had told me it was just a story made up by Miss Adele but now I was confused. It seemed that Mama and Little Charlie believed the dead born babies were in the castle. I was scared—really scared—but helpless till Poppa came home.

Poppa arrived home the next morning with his arms full of gifts. I ran to him and held him tight, not wanting him to ever leave again.

"Olivia, it's freezing in here. Why aren't the fires lit? It's colder in here than outside!"

"Poppa, Mama and Little Charlie are sick. I've been so worried and frightened. They stay in Little Charlie's room all the time and when Mama comes downstairs she says strange things."

"Where are they now, Olivia?"

"Like I said Poppa, up in Little Charlie's room with the door locked. She hasn't come downstairs at all today."

Poppa ran upstairs and knocked on the door. There was no sound from inside the room so Poppa pounded the door with his fist and yelled, "Open the door or I'm going to kick it in." A moment passed, then the sound of the key in the door lock. Mama stood there, her skin void of color, her eyes dark and sunken with sores all around her mouth. Poppa pushed past her and went to Little Charlie's bedside, reaching out to feel his forehead.

"What is going on? He's burning up with fever. Why haven't you taken him to a doctor? And the fires, why would you let the fires burn out? This house is like an icebox. No wonder he's sick!"

"A doctor can't help us. I was right. It's the house. This house with its thirteen rooms is killing us."

"Nonsense! You're as sick as Little Charlie. That's fever talking. I'm taking you both to the doctor now. Olivia, you go next door and stay with Miss Adele till we get back."

I was with Miss Adele for three days before Poppa's car pulled into the drive. Mama got out of the car but Little Charlie wasn't with her. Poppa leaned out the car window and waved at me then drove away. Mama still looked bad and even frailer. I asked her to take me to the hospital to see Little Charlie but she only smiled and said he's not in the hospital anymore; he's dancing with the Redbirds. I ran to the rock garden but he wasn't there; neither were the Redbirds. I checked the garden every day but Little Charlie was never there dancing. He never came home. Poppa never came home either.

Miss Adele started spending most of her time at the castle with Mama. When summer came they'd take their tea out to the rock garden and talk as I played nearby. Miss Adele would say, "You're better off forgetting him. Go on with your life. Land sakes, he didn't even come back to see his own son put in the ground. You need to look to Olivia, the one child you have left and forget about him."

Mama didn't listen; she started crying all the time. If she heard a sad story she cried, if she missed a speck of egg on a plate while washing dishes she cried. She cried about everything. Winter came with cold hard winds that seemed to blow even stronger through the walls of the castle than the winter before. Miss Adele sent her brother with loads of wood to fill the cellar and the secret passage. I kept a path clear in the hope that Little Charlie might come home in spite of what Mama said. Little Charlie didn't come, but snow did. It began to fall early morning. Mama watched through the windows and walked from one floor to the next. I heard her footsteps stop at the balcony door of the third floor. "Look what Mama has brought you," then I heard the door open and Mama's footsteps on the balcony porch.

I found her perched on the railing, a magazine page gripped in her hand, her feet half off the balcony rail. She forced her weight up and down on the rail as Little Charlie had done on the stairway the first day we came to the castle.

"Mama!"

"Yes, Olivia?"

"You should get down Mama. Come inside, it's cold out here."

"Mama is fine. You better put on a coat. It's snowing." A pebble on the roof above loosened by the snowfall fell to the balcony floor. Mama balanced on the rail looking down at the pebble.

"You see that, Olivia? Look at that Redbird dance." She tucked her arms to her chest, flapping her elbows up and down and lifted one foot from the rail.

"It's a sign Olivia. It's a sign. Go get Little Charlie. Hurry Olivia, it's time to dance with the Redbirds!" She opened the crumpled magazine page in her hand and held it out to me. It was a picture of a Cardinal perched on a limb with a bright blue sky and sun behind it. She smiled, "Hurry Olivia. Hurry." Then she was gone, over the rail.

#

I live with Miss Adele now. Sometimes she takes me to the cemetery at the end of the street to put flowers on the ground where she says Mama and Little Charlie are. Poppa sends me cards twice a year. Ten dollars for my birthday and twenty at Christmas. I don't remember what Poppa looks like. Sometimes I study the faces on the cards he sends and wonder if one of them might be Poppa's face. I asked Miss Adele but she said no, that none of them was Poppa. She said Poppa was nothing more than a devil. A devil that brought misery and pain to everything he ever touched. After that I drew horns on the heads of the people on the cards he sent and imagined he was one of the devils.

I think about Little Charlie and Mama all the time. I miss them. I told Miss Adele I wanted to be with them. Miss Adele said, "Don't be foolish child. You have a long, full life to lead. You don't want to be dead and in the ground like your Mama and Little Charlie."

Miss Adele tells stories. Stories that aren't always true. I don't believe they are in the ground. I know where Mama and Little Charlie are.

They're dancing. Dancing with the Redbirds.

Jan Fink

III.

Damon Pierce

The position of caseworker was an unexpected addition to the many tasks I did while working at a local thrift store and charitable organization. I'd had no formal training or previous background as a social worker but felt the work and ways of a charitable heart was worth doing. After being given a brief list of instructions as to what questions to ask, how to fill out the proper forms and how to assess the needs of clients, I was given the title of caseworker. The services we offered ranged from food baskets, temporary housing, Christmas for children, help with medication, power bills, housewares, school supplies, clothing and advice on how to budget a disability income.

The area reserved for casework consisted of a small section of the thrift store sales floor. A space outside the bathroom door had been partitioned off with curtain rods secured to the ceiling, then hung with shower curtains. There was enough room for a small desk and chair, a file cabinet and two chairs for clients. The Right of Privacy Act was laughable. Any thrift shopper browsing on the opposite side of the shower curtain could easily hear the intimate details of my clients' needs. Anyone in need of the restroom passed through my little office, bringing the interview to a halt till they relieved themselves, washed their hands and flushed. Then they once again passed through the office leaving me and the clients with the sound of a running toilet that had a tendency to keep going till I excused myself to tap the handle.

Even under these conditions I enjoyed my work. Over the next two years within the confines of my shower curtain office I was to see the best and the worst our society had to offer. There were the children who clung to my leg, looking up with smiling faces and thanking me for new school supplies and clothing. There were users of the system who sat across from me, eloquently lying about their income and situation. I saw the good hardworking souls down on their luck, the beaten, abused, frightened and deserted by their husbands or wives.

And there were the repeaters who had chosen charity as a way of life.

The hardest to deal with were the angry who lived on disability and made monthly car payments of five hundred dollars but couldn't feed or clothe their children. When denied assistance they shouted, cursed and threw anything they could find across the desk in my direction. After several of these incidents I took an intercom system that had been donated to the thrift store and set up a direct line to the cash register area. If things got out of hand I could push the call button and get help or a call to 911 would be made.

I'd be lying to you if I said I didn't become a little jaded as a caseworker. Early on I'd realized that to do this job you had to be caring and use judgment, but at the same time not be judgmental. The good cases that made your heart sing should have created a balance, but didn't. The faces of the abused, neglected and users of the system far outweighed the good, making it difficult to see the success of a charitable heart.

Day after day I would come home with my head filled with stories of need and sadness. It became hard to relate to my own family's need for conversation or solving their slightest problem. I was functioning on overload. There didn't seem to be any room left inside me. My husband gave my new position as caseworker a title of his own. He said I had become a sin eater.

My wise old Uncle made a statement many years ago that never left me. A neighbor of his had passed away and when I asked what took him my Uncle replied, "Sorriness. The man had been sorry all his life. Never worked, laid around and beat his wife and let his young'uns go hungry. He just got so sorry he died. Died of sorriness."

Many nights I had dreams of the street along my route to work. Dreams of the street being lined with bodies of people who had died of sorriness. I held my title of sin eater and handled thousands of cases through the years but never found the switch to empty myself. How do you throw up the woes of so many?

There is one case in particular I wish to share with you now. He came late in the afternoon, ten minutes before closing time. He was tall, extremely thin with skin the color of charcoal and wore ragged jeans and a worn suit coat. He entered my office uncertain, edgy, eyes wide and staring with dilated pupils that floated in a pool of red where the whites of his eyes should have been. I suspected drugs or drink, maybe both. I asked him to take a seat, which he reluctantly did after a quick glance around the small enclosure. I took out the paperwork and began the interview by asking what assistance he needed.

"I'm hungry."

"Your name sir?"

"Damon Pierce. Damon Pierce. Damon Pierce."

He repeated his name once more in quick short spurts, his voice lower this time as he looked at the photos of my children along the office wall behind me.

"Your address?"

"Aint got one."

"Your age?"

He pulled at a loose thread in the collar of the suit coat. The thread unraveled freely and he continued to pull, wrapping its length around his little finger.

"Your age?"

"We aint gonna get into that. You got pretty fingernails. They're pretty the way you got them all squared off like that on the ends."

"Sir, in order to help you today we have to have this information."

He was still pulling at the thread, wrapping his finger, half the right side of his suit collar now unraveled. Then he stopped and turned his attention back to me.

"Don't know. I aint old and I aint young."

He tapped his temple with the thread wrapped finger, his face turning childlike. I made a guess at his age and entered the number on the form, then went on to the next question.

"What is your situation?"

He looked at me, a blank stare on his face. It was clear he didn't understand. I rephrased the question.

"What has happened in your life that brought you here for help?"

He rose from his chair, slammed the palms of his hands down hard on the desk and leaned toward me. That close he smelled of rust. The scent you find in old tin cans left in heaps to oxidize in wet, abandoned fields.

"Fathers killing mothers, mothers killing fathers, mothers killing daughters, daughters killing mothers, sisters killing sisters, brothers killing brothers, babies killing babies!"

He preached this to the air, his breath filling the small office. Breath that smelled of turned wine and dried blood. I reached for the intercom call button but didn't press it. I realized I felt no fear of this man. As he spoke, his eyes didn't see me, he was somewhere else, far from this makeshift office. It was over quickly. He became silent and sat down heavily in the chair across from me.

"I'm hungry."

"Wait here, Mr. Pierce."

I tossed his paperwork in the waste basket and went to the food pantry to collect his groceries. I filled the box with three of each variety of canned meats and vegetables, bread, crackers, bottled water and sweet cakes. On the sales floor I added a can opener, skillet, pots and pans, odd silverware and matches. If he was homeless he could at least build a fire and have a hot meal.

"Mr. Pierce, I have your food ready."

"Damon Pierce. Damon Pierce. Damon Pierce."

He chanted his name, holding on to the one piece of real information he knew, then stood and reached out for the box. Then he hesitated, plunging his hands into the pockets of his jeans. His fingers fumbled the contents of his left pocket, turning it inside out, his hand coming out empty. Then he tried his right pocket and pulled out a handful of lint, a few small stones and four pennies. He held them out to me in a shaking hand.

"This is to help you. You don't have to give me anything."

He cupped his hand, placed it gently on my desk and opened his fist, dropping the lint, stones and pennies. Only then did he reach out and take the box.

"Are you going to be all right?"

For the first time since he entered my office he looked me straight in the eyes.

"Is the world right?"

"Sometimes."

For a moment his face lost that faraway look, his charcoal skin softened and his eyes cleared, losing a little of the redness that filled them. He smiled for a few moments and walked to the door.

I no longer do casework, but my days as a sin eater will always be with me. Out of all those cases I think of Damon Pierce the most. It is always his smile that comes to mind. The smile that came from a tortured body and soul. A smile that made me realize how little I truly knew of the world I had tried to help through a charitable heart.

Damon Pierce had knowledge. He knew things I would never know or completely understand. He knew the world wasn't right and that it may never be right. And just maybe when he spoke of fathers killing mothers, mothers killing fathers, mothers killing daughters, daughters killing mothers, sisters killing sisters, brothers killing brothers, babies killing babies, he knew of death by sorriness. He had offered up all he had in payment for a box of food, fearing death by sorriness might also be his fate. That day long ago, his parting smile defined misery for me.

Misery was Damon Pierce, Damon Pierce, Damon Pierce.

Jan Fink

IV.

Clara Jean

The first time I saw Clara Jean I was on an errand for Mama. Ever since the scare of Y2K, Mama had been obsessed with security. After that uneventful part of world history Mama lived in a state of hysterics, demanding constant security upgrades. She convinced herself that just because it didn't happen in the year 2000, it could still happen any day now.

Mama was hunched over the kitchen table that morning, gripping the stub of a number two pencil, busy writing down her new list on a sheet of notebook paper. Before I could pour myself a cup of coffee she was on me, shoving the list and a hundred dollar bill in my hand.

"You got to go get these things for me today. Things are going to be bad, son. People breaking down our doors to take what little we have, and maybe even worse."

I glanced over the list: new deadbolt locks for the front and back door, locks for all the windows, shells for Daddy's old shotgun and motion-sensor lights for the yard. As security goes, the list of items was impressive, but I couldn't understand Mama's concern. We didn't have anything worth the trouble for someone to knock down our door and take. The house was decorated with thrift and dime store junk. The only item of any value that came to my mind was Mama's Marilyn Monroe scrapbook. Now, that might be worth the trouble. Mama was not one to argue with so I took the list and folded hundred dollar bill she handed me and drove downtown to the hardware store.

Clara Jean was standing there behind the cash register ringing up a box of rat poison. I'd never seen her around town before. If I had, believe me, I would have remembered. She was just about the prettiest woman I'd had the occasion to see. Clara Jean was a tiny little thing, with skin the color of those white China plates you see on the Martha Stewart Living Show. Not that I watch such shows, but once when Mama had the television tuned in to that channel I passed through the living room and Mama pointed out the beautiful China plates

Martha was using that day to serve up a piece of roasted chicken. That's how I knew at first glance Clara Jean had skin like fine China. It wasn't just her skin that held my attention. Her hair made my knees weak. She had lots of it and she wore it teased up high around her small face. High and blond as corn silk, that was Clara Jean's hair.

I went about my shopping, taking my time, looking down at Mama's list and looking up at Clara Jean. While I was in the ammo aisle she caught me looking at her and she gave me a quick smile with her tiny pink lips. My knees damn near gave way on me and it was somewhere along the aisle among the ammo that I lost Mama's list and could not for the life of me remember what else I was there to pick up.

I wish I could tell you about going to the register with my purchases, but I don't remember much about checking out. You see, when I got that close to Clara Jean I could smell her hair. It smelled of sweet, fresh green apples and that's all I remember till I got home and Mama brought me around fussing about the missing window locks and motion-sensor lights. I made up a story.

"Sorry Mama, the hardware was out of them. I'll try back next week to see if they got any in stock." Then to ease her a little I started installing the new deadbolt on the front door. As I worked I brought up seeing a new face at the hardware. I told

Mama she was real pretty and seemed nice and that I might ask her out for dinner.

"What does this girl look like?"

"She's tiny, pale skinned with pretty blond hair."

"Does she wear that pretty blond hair all ratted up high on her head?"

"Yeah, something like that."

"Good Lord! That's Clara Jean you're talking about. Clara Jean Watson! I didn't know she was back in town. Well son, that's one young lady—and I use the term lightly—that you can put right out of your mind. She's nothing but trouble! Her whole family is nothing but trouble. This town gave a sigh of relief when they up and left years ago and now she's back like a bad stray dog that wore out its welcome some other place. She's come back to pick up where she left off—begging and swindling anyone fool enough to give her a look. You're not going to take her to dinner. You just get her out of your mind, you hear? You hear me? Put her clean out of your mind!"

I heard Mama, but I couldn't get Clara Jean out of my mind. I thought of her as I installed the deadbolts, loaded Daddy's shotgun, through dinner and long into the night. When I was certain Mama was asleep, I crept quietly into the living room and opened the large pine wardrobe where Mama kept her

Marilyn Monroe scrapbook. I took it from the top shelf and back to bed with me, looking over Marilyn's photos till the sky began to lighten in my window, then returned it before Mama woke. There was no doubt in my mind. Clara Jean looked just like Marilyn. No matter what Mama said I had to have Clara Jean Watson.

I made a dozen trips to the hardware in less than two weeks but never spoke a word to Clara Jean while she rang up my items at the register. It was Friday the thirteenth of that second week that Clara Jean gave me another smile when I put my purchases on the counter.

"You shop here a lot. What's your name?"

"Love. I mean my name is John Love." She continued to bag my items, looking up at me smiling.

"You're kidding me. I never met anyone with the last name Love. That your real name, John Love?"

"Yeah. Real name. All my life."

"Well that is just about the most delightful name I ever heard of. John Love, you sure do buy a lot of hardware."

"It's part of my work. I own a handyman business. I use a lot of hardware in the handyman business."

"Huh. You own your own handyman business. How fascinating. I've heard a handyman can fix just about anything. That true John Love? Can you fix anything?"

"So far I haven't run up on anything I couldn't put back together and make better. Maybe you might want to go out for dinner sometimes and I could tell you about my work."

"John Love, you got perfect timing. Just so happens I'm free tomorrow night. Pick me up at seven?" She flashed me that sweet smile with those tiny pink lips and my heart was singing when she pressed a small piece of paper with her address written on it into my palm.

Our date was a day away, but I drove past her house as soon as I left the hardware store to make sure I could find it. The address was on the west side of town. The house number she gave took me to a rundown plantation home that a single family probably couldn't afford to keep up and had been converted into apartments. There was a large faded wooden sign out front on the lawn with the words, "Dixie Apartments" "Only Three Vacancies Left" written in peeling black paint." It seemed right that Clara Jean would live in such a house. Sweet, gentle, beautiful Clara Jean bringing back grace to the ruins of days of glorious Southern living.

The remainder of that day and much of the next I spent cleaning my truck, getting a haircut, shining my shoes and going through my closet looking for the right shirt and pants. I was convinced Mama knew what I was doing, but if she did, she never said one word. She just sat and watched me with no emotion on her face. I felt a little guilty about keeping a secret, going against her wishes and sorry for Mama at the same time. Daddy had been dead now for almost ten years and other than old June Tremblay who lived down the street I was all Mama had in her life. I loved Mama but at that moment I loved Clara Jean more. I was to pick up Clara Jean at seven, but my nerves got the best of me so I left early and drove around for forty-five minutes before knocking on her door. Her apartment was on the second floor and what a vision she was, standing there framed in the doorway like a picture of Marilyn.

She was wearing a tight pink dress, the exact same pink as her lips. A print of small red roses ran along the neckline and down across her left breast. Pink dress, red roses, smiling pink lips, fine China skin and her hair smelling of fresh, sweet green apples. I was a lucky man.

She told me Dairy Queen was her favorite place to eat so I drove down Main Street to the restaurant and parked close to the door as a gentleman should. We chose a nice booth in the corner and ordered burgers, fries and shakes. As we ate Clara

Jean talked of her family and how they had drifted out of town because of certain misfortunes that befell them. Misfortunes she said she didn't feel comfortable sharing with me on a first date.

"I just got up one day and left. Not that they cared one little bit. My Mama and Daddy were so cruel to me and even now they don't contribute a penny toward my welfare. But you see this town has always been home to me so naturally I wanted to come back here. So I'm on my own now and working at the hardware to make ends meet and stay alive. Some days I don't want to get up in the mornings, but I have plans. I don't want to work behind a cash register the rest of my life. I plan to go back to school and learn computers. There are all kinds of good jobs sitting at a desk if you know computers."

I could have sat there in that booth listening to her talk all night. My heart went out to her. Clara Jean, such a small sweet thing with dreams and all alone in the world. When I dropped her at her door I tried to kiss her. Oh, I know I shouldn't have on a first date, but I couldn't help myself. I wanted to taste those pink lips so badly, but she turned her cheek. She smiled with those pink lips, raised her China hand and stroked my cheek. "I'm sorry Honey. I never kiss without first brushing my teeth."

No kiss, but she did agree to go out with me again after work the next day. "I'd be delighted to go back to the Dairy Queen with you since that is my most favorite eating establishment in the whole wide world." I left her there smiling and waving, framed in the doorway, went home, pulled out the Marilyn scrapbook and counted off the minutes of the coming twenty-four hours till I'd see her again.

On our second date, Clara Jean ordered the large Blitz Burger Combo with extra fries, onion rings and a side of coleslaw. She cleaned her plate. I was wondering how such a tiny little thing could hold so much food when the waitress arrived at our table and Clara Jean ordered coffee and a banana spilt. When her dessert came Clara Jean reached into her purse and pulled out a Fingerhut catalog. She flashed that smile with her pink lips.

"There's something I want to show you." She thumbed through the pages of the catalog with her left hand and ate her banana split with her right. When she found the page she was searching for she pushed the catalog across the table to me. She tapped page fifty two with four of her red polished nails.

"See that? That's a computer. That's just the thing I need to get out from behind the cash register at the hardware." I didn't have knowledge as far as computers went so I took her word for it.

"You know, sweetheart, that's the very thing I need till I can get myself in school. You know what I mean, practice—and who knows, I might not even need to go to school if I had this. I could teach myself and save all that tuition. The payments are only thirty-nine dollars and sixty-nine cents a month, but I don't have any credit. I'd be so delighted to have one of these — course even on credit I couldn't afford a measly thirty-nine dollars and sixty-nine cents a month on the salary the hardware pays me."

Clara Jean sighed and turned her attention back to the banana split. She had called me sweetheart. Those pink lips called me sweetheart. I told her to order the computer, put it in my name and I'd make the payments till she got on her feet.

"Really?" Those pink lips smiling as she reached across the table and took my hand. "Why John Love, you are just the sweetest man that ever was!"

At her door that night I tried to kiss her goodnight, but she turned her cheek. I told her it didn't bother me that her teeth weren't brushed but she declined the kiss anyway saying, "John Love, honey, you know I had onion rings with dinner and I would simply die before I'd offend you with a kiss with onion on my breath." That's okay, I thought. Clara Jean was worth the wait.

We began seeing each other every night of the week. Our dates were always at the Dairy Queen and the Fingerhut catalog was always on the table. She had so many needs, poor thing with no help from her Mama and Daddy. As her gentleman suitor I felt obliged to help her with her needs. She needed cookware, dishes and silverware so she could cook me good homemade meals. And she added that a stereo system with a CD player in a nice oak cabinet so we could listen to romantic music as we dined would just be delightful.

"All of that for seventy-nine dollars and ninety-nine cents a month. Can you believe what a bargain that is, sweetheart?"

To date I'd never been past her front door, but now I could picture in my mind UPS delivering the dishes, cookware, silverware and stereo and her calling me to come for our romantic dinner. I'd bring roses and after dinner she'd brush her teeth and we'd kiss and I'd hold her tightly in my arms and before I knew it I'd said yes.

"Clara Jean, you fill out that Fingerhut order form as soon as I drop you by home. I'll make the payments."

Four weeks passed, and during our nightly dinner at Dairy Queen I asked her if her order had arrived. She picked up her napkin and dabbed the corners of her mouth. "Yes, it arrived, but you know what sweetheart? After I put away my cookware, dishes, silverware and set up the stereo, I looked around my living room and realized there was no way I could invite a gentleman like you over for a romantic dinner. My sofa and arm chairs are so worn the springs are showing right through the fabric and I don't even have so much as an end table or coffee table. Now how could I possibly serve you a nice bottle of wine and a tray of appetizers before dinner with not so much as a coffee table to set it on? No sweetheart, I just can't bring myself to have you over knowing I couldn't entertain you properly."

A single tear made its way down that China face and the catalog made its way across the table. There on page sixty seven was a glossy picture of a living room suite. I was beginning to think there was nothing a body could desire that couldn't be ordered from a Fingerhut catalog. The living room suite was delivered six weeks later.

For months now I'd spent every evening out with Clara Jean and Mama didn't seem the wiser as to where I was going every night. With the nightly meals at the Dairy Queen, the extra gas it took traveling back and forth to the west side of town and my monthly payments of over one hundred dollars a month to Fingerhut I was running short of money. Asking Mama to cut my hair was my first mistake. She began to question me as to where my money was going so fast that I couldn't afford a haircut. I avoided her questions till a few weeks later when I had no choice but to admit where my money was going.

Mama's friend June Tremblay was having dinner at the Dairy Queen and saw me and Clara Jean in our booth. June went straight home, rang Mama up on the phone and told her all she'd seen and suspected. That was all Mama needed to hear. She was waiting for me when I got home and it all hit the fan.

"I warned you! I told you about Clara Jean Watson and what do you do? You go out with her anyway and let her take every penny you work hard to make. I'm glad your poor Daddy is in the ground already because this would kill him for sure. Clara Jean Watson is a sorry piece of flesh just like her Mama and Daddy. Ever one of them grifters! That girl will take your very breath away and your poor old Mama's breath too if you keep this up."

I kept quiet. There was no need to argue because nothing was going to change. I was going to keep seeing Clara Jean and there was not a damn thing Mama could do about it. There was only one part of what Mama said that night about Clara Jean that I agreed with. Clara Jean did take my very breath away, and one day I would have her.

I'd been seeing Clara Jean for over a year now and she still needed so much. Each month brought a new Fingerhut catalog, new needs and new orders. My monthly payments were up to six hundred dollars. I was so short of money I ordered grilled cheese and water at the Dairy Queen each night and let Clara

Jean do most of the eating. This she did well and never showed an extra pound in her effort. I was losing weight. I'd never had a case of nerves in my life but lately I felt on edge and tired all the time. Life at home with Mama didn't help. She had all but forgotten her obsession with home security and focused totally on me. It wasn't so much what she said; she rarely spoke to me at all anymore. It was the way she looked at me — like I was a dead man walking.

Then one morning at breakfast she slammed my bowl of oatmeal down on the kitchen table and said, "Clara Jean Watson didn't even have to go to the trouble of knocking down our door to take everything we got. You invited her in. She's got all your money and now she's taking your very breath away and your Mama's breath too."

They were the last words Mama spoke to me. I spent my time with Clara Jean and Mama spent her time in front of the television, smoking one Camel after another and sipping strong iced tea. This went on till the end of winter. I got home late that night, the heat was off and the house dark. I could hear the television in the living room; Jay Leno was introducing Jack Hannah and the audience applauding. I called out but got no answer. Mama was in her chair in front of the set with a burned down Camel between her fingers. The ice in her tea was melted and Mama's breath was gone.

I was grateful that Mama had a burial policy. The service was short, a few words, couple of flower arrangements, me, June Tremblay and a handful of neighbors in attendance. Clara Jean couldn't make the service.

"Sorry Hon, it's inventory time at the hardware and I just have to stay and get it done. And of course we can skip our dinner at Dairy Queen tonight. You can pick me up at seven tomorrow night and tell me about your poor Mama's service. I'll miss you tonight sweetheart." Then she was off down the hardware aisle with a wide rule tablet and a pencil in her hand, counting drill bits. I understood her not wanting to come to the funeral. They'd never met but Mama knew a lot about Clara Jean, and according to Mama none of it was good. Clara Jean was probably afraid she wouldn't be welcome at the service, but it still would have been nice to have her by my side at the funeral.

Mama and I hadn't been on good terms for a long time before she passed, but I found that I missed her more than I thought I would. I took her Zippo lighter, slipped it in my jeans pocket and carried it with me everywhere. I took the Marilyn scrapbook from the wardrobe and kept it on my bedside table, thumbing through the pages nightly and thinking of beautiful Clara Jean. The first day of spring she showed me her newest need from Fingerhut. It was a feather bed mattress topper.

"It'd be like sleeping on a cloud," she said, and added that she'd need new sheet sets, probably queen size to compensate for the extra thickness the topper would create and a new comforter too. Of course I told her to place the order. I took the last bite of my grilled cheese and held my breath, hoping that was all her needs for the evening. Three weeks later the phone rang and there was Clara Jean's sweet voice on the line inviting me to dinner at her apartment. It was finally happening. Wine, appetizers, romantic music, then dinner, then she'd brush her teeth and oh God I'd kiss her, hold her, make love to her, ask her to marry me and be mine forever.

I felt good, energized. Called the florist and ordered two dozen roses, pulled the thrift store suit I'd bought for Mama's funeral from the pine wardrobe, shined my shoes, thought about the ring I'd put on her finger and even washed the dishes that were always piling up since Mama left. The minutes of the day ticked by slowly; six o'clock seemed an eternity away. I had to get away from the clock, stay busy. I went to the jewelry store on Main and found a silver ring with a small cubic zirconia setting, charged it, went back home and cut the grass that was knee high. Four o'clock I showered and tried on the suit. The jacket hung off my shoulders. I'd lost more weight. I decided just the suit pants and a nice button down shirt and tie would have to do. Five o'clock and I've picked up the roses, the ring in my pants pocket and I'm standing at her door thirty minutes early and hesitant to knock. Five minutes pass—feels like five hours—so I go ahead and tap the door lightly. The door opens and she's standing there in the same pink dress with the print of small red roses along the neckline and down her left breast that she'd worn on our first date.

"Oh my, you're early, Love. That's gonna be my new nickname for you. Course it's not really a nickname cause it's your real name. Works out well, don't you agree Love? Well don't just stand there Love; come in." I nodded my head and stepped into her apartment, handing her the roses.

"Roses for me Love? I just might cry Love!" She didn't cry but rushed off to the kitchen for a vase, telling me to help myself to the wine and appetizers she'd set out on the coffee table. I pour two glasses of wine and nibble on crackers and cheese as Clara Jean carries the conversation from the kitchen, talking about how delightful and breathtaking the roses are and how she hoped she had a vase worthy to put them in. As she went on about the roses I look around the room. The stereo in its fine oak cabinet is playing soft piano music. The shipping box that held the computer sits in the corner unopened. Guess Clara Jean hadn't gotten around to practicing her computer skills. The new sofa was comfortable, elegant, and finer than anything my poor Mama ever owned. So was the coffee table, end tables and other items throughout the room. Looking at them, every monthly payment I was making slowly came back to me from the glossy photos of the Fingerhut catalog.

Clara Jean was still talking when she came back to the living room and placed the vase of roses on the coffee table next to the appetizers. She picked up her glass of wine and sat down in one of the big arm chairs across from me. "Love, hon, you look deep in thought. Everything okay? Dinner's ready, I thought we'd dine out here in the living room. Is that good with you?"

"Yeah, I'm okay and dinner in the living room is fine." That's what I said to Clara Jean, but I wasn't okay. I felt odd. The surge of energy I'd carried all day had up and left. Dinner was awkward with Clara Jean doing most of the talking. I don't even remember what she served or if I ate. My head was full of numbers, my mind trying to calculate the payments, the total cost of everything in that living room and how the hell I'd ever pay it off. The total cost was up to thousands not including the ring I'd charged today, and I was still counting when Clara Jean took my hand.

"Stand up and close your eyes. I have a surprise for you." I obey and she begins leading me. "Just a little further down the hall. Keep those eyes closed." I hear a door open. "Open eyes wide Love!"

When my vision clears we are in her bedroom. This is it. This is what I've waited for. Clara Jean. Clara Jean. I should take her in my arms now, take the ring from my pocket and… She skips to the bed and jumps onto the new feather mattress topper. But that's not all that's new. Catalog glossy flashbacks from page ten, eleven and twelve or was it thirteen, fourteen and fifteen. A new four poster bed, bedside tables, lamps and a wing back chair in the corner and I don't remember telling Clara Jean it was okay to order them.

I stood in the doorway watching her roll back and forth on that cloud of softness and I thought of Mama sleeping her whole life in an old iron bed with a lumpy mattress. Clara Jean looked like a China angel on a cloud and I should have taken the ring from my pocket and put it on her finger but I felt ill. Sweat covered my brow and ran down my cheeks. The palms of my hands were burning and there was a stirring in me that made me turn away from her. I began to tremble. I'd like to tell you it was passion but it wasn't. It was something else, something that frightened me, made my stomach churn and made me stumbling weak.

"Love, you look terrible! What's wrong?" I mumble that I'm not feeling well and should go home and rest. "Oh, I hope it wasn't the tuna casserole. You never know about canned tuna. Yes, Love you go home and get some rest. I'll see you tomorrow night when you pick me up. Same time, seven right?"

I made it to my truck and up came the tuna casserole. Guess I did eat something at dinner. All I could think of on the way home was the old wooden box Daddy kept out in the garage. It was stored in the far right corner with a pile of tarps, broken saws and hoe handles on top of it. Daddy kept a bottle of Southern Comfort in it and would visit the box four, sometimes five days a week. More if Mama was in a spell and on his case about one thing or another. Nothing in the garage had been touched since Daddy died so I was sure it was still there, a little comfort that I could hold in my hand and pour down my throat. I needed that comfort now. I needed to shake this sick, gut-wrenching feeling that I couldn't put a name to or understand why it was happening.

Home at last and I'm stumbling up the drive on legs that insist on failing me. Halfway to the garage another wave of nausea hits and up comes more tuna casserole. A fit of giggles came on and I screamed into the dark, "GET IT TOGETHER! GET IT TOGETHER JOHN LOVE!"

More giggles, now I'm really losing it, out here in the dark talking to myself. I right myself, stagger the few more feet to the garage, open the door and flip the light switch. It's still there. I grab the bottom tarp and with one pull send the broken saws and hoe handles clattering to the floor around my feet. The effort makes me dizzy; I lean against the box till my head clears then open the lid. Work gloves, dozens of mismatched, stained, ripped gloves that must have taken Daddy years to accumulate. I dig down in the box, tossing gloves over my shoulder and halfway down my fingers find it. I hold it up to the light. The label had deteriorated and now spelled out "outhern Comfort" but that didn't matter, there was three quarters of the bottle left, plenty of comfort for me.

I take my comfort inside, go to the living room and plop down in Mama's chair. Taking a long draw from the bottle I pick up the remote and flip channels till I find The Tonight Show. A half pack of Mama's Camels is still on the TV tray next to the chair. I pull the Zippo from my pocket and the ring box comes out with it, falling to the floor. I leave it on the floor, light up a Camel and take another draw of comfort. The Camel is stale, bitter tasting but goes down well with the whiskey. I drink, smoke and doze while Leno drones out one liners and introductions.

"And tonight before we bring out our first guest, I've just been handed a message for John Love. So John, if you're out there watching, here it is." I'm suddenly wide awake, trying to focus my blurred vision. Leno leans in to the camera, his face filling up the television screen.

"John Love, your Mama wants you to know that Clara Jean Watson is taking your very breath away. Don't go away folks, Harrison Ford coming right up."

It was late afternoon the next day when I woke with a hangover, the television still playing, ashtray full of Camel butts and the empty bottle of "outhern Comfort" lying on the floor next to the ring box. I remembered Leno reading the message but Mama couldn't have sent that message to The Tonight Show. It had to be Daddy's whiskey gone bad after years in the garage, and I'd spent the night pouring every damn bit of it down my throat. Leno didn't read that message, it was bad whiskey hallucinations. The phone rings, setting off an explosion in my head. It's Clara Jean. I let the answering machine get it. I'd be seeing her tonight at the Dairy Queen.

I stumble to the kitchen, take the last two tablespoons of coffee and brew up a weak pot. The first cup comes right back up. I stand at the sink gagging and wondering how much worse my health could possibly get. My weight was down from two hundred twenty five to one hundred sixty and my Fingerhut payments were up from six hundred fifty a month to one thousand. My handyman jobs had all but played out. I couldn't concentrate, made too many mistakes and lost customers. Mama left me her life savings of five thousand dollars but that was going fast toward the Fingerhut payments.

The weight loss was bad enough, but for the last two months I'd developed a constant twitch in my right eye. If Clara Jean had noticed it she never brought it up.

My head is still throbbing at dinner that night. Clara Jean sits across from me eating her combo and talking with those pretty pink lips. Lips I have yet to kiss. She talks and eats and I watch her lips, not really hearing what she's saying. The waitress brings her banana split and Clara Jean picks up her spoon and pushes the catalog across the table.

"Love, Fingerhut has a new item this month. It's called Aromatherapy. Oh, it's the latest thing, sweetheart. The complete set has bath salts, lotions, massage oil and even candles that we could use at dinner the next time I cook for you. It says here in the catalog description that Aromatherapy soothes the senses and relieves the pressures of everyday life. Don't know if you've noticed, hon, but standing at that cash register day in and day out at the hardware just takes so much out of me. I am so stressed some days I think I'll just die. And look—the whole set of products is just one hundred fifty dollars—with easy monthly payments of course."

I look down at the glossy display of candles, magic bottles, potions for the soul to relieve the stresses of the body and mind and a surge of power over takes me. I look up at Clara Jean, her pink lips still moving, big corn silk, fresh green apple-smelling hair and I shout into her China plate face.

"SHUT UP CLARA JEAN WATSON! YOU TOOK MY MAMA'S BREATH AWAY AND DAMN NEAR TOOK MINE TOO!"

Clara Jean's eyes went wide. The Dairy Queen went silent, people in the surrounding booths turned and stared in our direction. Clara Jean sat there frozen, mouth open with a spoon of her banana split halfway raised to her lips. I bolt over the table, grab her by the shoulders, lift her and kiss her hard on those pink lips. I release her and she plops down in the booth, the spoon of ice cream falling to her lap.

I pick up the Fingerhut catalog, pull Mama's Zippo from my pocket and light the damn thing, dropping it into Clara Jean's banana split. I glance back only once as I leave. Waitresses are emptying water glasses on the burning catalog. Clara Jean is crying and holding back her high teased corn silk hair to keep it from igniting.

I go home feeling better than I have in a long time. I make myself a sandwich, turn on the television and sit in Mama's chair with the Marilyn scrapbook. Mama's reading glasses are on the TV tray; I put them on and study Marilyn's photos carefully.

You know ... Clara Jean Watson didn't look a bit like Marilyn.

Jan Fink

V.

Greenland

I can't tell you what I look like. I look in the mirror and see nothing but space. Space reflecting space, that's what the mirror shows. It figures because Grandmamma said I was nothing but dirt. Dirt under her feet she'd say. Dirt she needed to keep kicking out of the way. Grandmamma said I wasn't sweeping-up kind of dirt; I was the kind of dirt you needed to kick and scrape off the bottom of your shoes.

She always had a way of making me feel worthwhile. Even if I was dirt I had a purpose if for nothing else than to collect on the bottoms of her shoes. Looking back I suppose I kept Grandmamma up and going. It took a lot of energy for her to keep on kicking me.

I quit looking in the mirror, but sometimes when Grandmamma was feeling the spirit, she'd take me by my shoulders and stand me in front of her looking glass and ask me what I saw. When I didn't reply she shook me till I said, "Nothing."

Then she'd shake me harder, saying, "You better look again, boy. Don't you see your sins? Don't you see the sinner you are, Little Bill? Do you see the sinner in that mirror?" I'd finally give in and nod my head yes but I didn't see nothing in that mirror.

Mama and I lived with Grandmamma. She owned a two-story run-down house and a hundred acres along the bank of the Alabama River. The house and land had been passed down through generations. Mama said all the family died off and there was no one left to leave it to but Grandmamma. The house stayed in disrepair, wood rotting with badly sealed doors and windows that let in the cold and dampness. Grandmamma hired a few men to do some of the work but the minute one of them looked at Mama or she learned they smoked or had an occasional drink she sent them packing. She never found a worker that didn't take to one temptation or another so the house was let be.

Grandmamma hated the river and would have been happy if it dried up or could route itself along someone else's land. She never went down to the river and I was forbidden to go there. She said the river had taken her son and husband and she wished it had taken old Rouse too. Rouse was Granddaddy's hunting dog and Grandmamma said he was the only one that came back from the river that day. She kept Rouse chained to the back porch post, didn't feed him much and often said she wished he'd go on and die. I loved the river. Every chance I got I'd unchain Rouse and we'd go down to the river's edge and wade in the shallows, and I'd listen to the fast middle current rushing its way through the land. It was my place of beauty and peace, the banks full of lush green plants and tall water oaks. Sometimes I tried to imagine where the river had taken Grandmamma's son and husband. I thought that wherever the river had taken them it was probably a nice place.

As early as I can remember, Mama came and went. Sometimes she'd be gone a couple of days and sometimes she didn't come home for weeks. I never knew when she'd be back but I always knew when she was leaving. She'd do her hair, put on makeup, one of her best dresses and high heels, and pack a small leather bag. She never said goodbye, just walked out the door and down the lane to a waiting car. Every time Mama left, Grandmamma would lock herself in her bedroom upstairs and play old recordings of gospel hymns on her phonograph. While the hymns played she would pray in a loud weeping voice. It was the same voice Grandmamma used at funerals and gravesides, a voice that shouted to the heavens the glory of God and Jesus. Then she'd weep and shout to the heavens some more. She'd stay up there for days shouting out in that unsettling voice that frightened me.

In my mind I'd try to block out the days when Mama was gone and Grandmamma was holed up in prayer but the only thing that really helped was going to the river with old Rouse. I'd pack us picnics of thick slices of buttered bread and honey and we'd eat at the river's edge, watching the hawks swoop down diving for minnows and frogs. Mama was gone my first day of school; she had been gone for over a month this time. I was a little scared that morning when Grandmamma told me to walk to the end of the lane and wait for a big yellow bus that would take me five miles down the road to Riverside Elementary. There were a lot of kids on the bus all talking and laughing but I took a seat by myself and kept quiet. I wasn't used to being around anybody, shy and timid to the point of being nonexistent.

I didn't make any friends in my class and most times when the teacher called on me for anything I could barely mumble an answer. I had trouble with my lessons and couldn't read the simplest letter or sentence, but I enjoyed the books the school allowed me to bring home. I looked at the pictures for hours on end imagining the stories the images told. There were pictures of pretty houses, animals, happy children with mothers and fathers that made me want to go into the page and be a part of the picture and never come back out.

The third week of school my bus driver said, "Little Bill, you don't have much to say. Was your daddy's name Bill? Is that why you're called Little Bill?" I told her I didn't know but I'd ask my grandmamma. I waited till the next day after school to bring up the question. Grandmamma was at the stove lifting pieces of battered chicken from a skillet of oil with a long two-pronged fork. As she moved the pieces to different locations in the skillet she hummed then sang out the words to "Amazing Grace." I sat and watched her. She seemed happy so I thought it would be the right time to ask her about my daddy.

"Grandmamma, since my name is Little Bill, was my daddy's name Bill? The bus driver asked me yesterday if I was named after my daddy and I told her I'd ask you cause I wasn't sure. Was my daddy's name Bill?"

She turned so quickly I didn't have time to react. She hit me in the face hard enough to knock me from my chair to the floor and then stood over me with the fork raised, dripping hot oil down the outside of her arm and on to the front of my shirt. Her eyes were wild, full of rage and contempt.

"Get up! Get up off that floor and back in that chair!"

I tried to get up but all I could manage was weaving back and forth on my hands and knees. I'd seen Rouse in this same position, weaving and staggering, trying to stand up after Grandmamma hit him with a heavy pot for getting off his chain. I felt a warm trickle run down my upper lip and into my mouth, the taste salty and bitter. I still couldn't get to my feet, my head spinning, so she landed a kick to my chin. More blood falling to the kitchen floor in red sun-splattered drops. I began sobbing.

"You cry and it'll only make this harder. I told you to get up off the floor and back in that chair! Now! Now! Now! Why can't you listen and do as you're told?" She jabbed the fork into my shoulder and then pulled me up, dragging me to the stove, where she held my hand to the hot skillet. The pain was so unbearable I screamed and that made her even madder. She pulled me across the room and pushed me down in the kitchen chair screaming at me.

"Shut up! Shut up or you'll get more!" She stood over me with the fork raised. I reached up to wipe away the blood that was flowing from my nose and chin.

"Don't touch that. That's your sacrifice, your key to redemption. Now you listen to me. You didn't have no daddy.

You had a father. You want to know your father's name? Your father's name is Jesus, Jesus Christ our Lord. That's your father's name! And as far as that meddling school bus driver is concerned that's what you're going to tell her the next time you get on the bus. Is that clear? Did you hear me, Little Bill?" I nodded yes.

"Little Bill, there's a difference between a father and a daddy. Jesus sent you down to your mama to punish her. My Judith was clean and pure before you. Since Jesus sent you for that reason, you have to be good and free of evil or suffer redemption punishment. Now you're going to get back down on your hands and knees and clean up my floor. After we eat we're going to pray for your redemption."

She went to the sink, wet a dishcloth and tossed it to me. Then she went back to the skillet, taking the fork that still had my blood on it, and turned the chicken pieces one by one. She began to hum, happy again. I got down on my hands and knees and began cleaning up the red suns I'd dropped on the floor. With each wipe of the dishcloth the suns became swirls then smears of red on the white linoleum. Blood continued to flow from my nose, chin and shoulder, dripping to the floor, making new suns of crimson, the wet dishcloth turning them into new beautiful designs. I don't know how long I had been there making art with my own blood when she finally called me back to the table. The chicken was arranged on a platter with the two-pronged fork stuck in the top piece. I sat in my blood soaked clothing, eating the chicken, and waited for the time I would pray for my redemption with Grandmamma.

I missed three weeks of school. My teacher called the second week and I heard Grandmamma on the phone talking in her nice happy voice.

"You know how boys are. Little Bill is constantly doing something he's got no business doing. He climbed a big pine out back of the house and fell right out of it. And the very next day he grabbed a hot skillet trying to get a piece of chicken and burned his hand. He busted his nose and chin pretty bad in the fall and he's got a bad burn on his hand, but I think he'll be healed enough in another week to get back to school. I sure do appreciate you calling to check on him."

I spent a lot of time missing school, watching Mama come and go and down on my knees with Grandmamma praying for redemption. I was a sinner. Even with all the missed school days I got better at learning my lessons and enjoyed every day I got to attend. My teacher taught us a lesson about a country called Greenland. I don't remember much about the lesson, but I liked the name; it reminded me of the banks along the river where Rouse and I went to play. I found an old piece of wood in the barn, took my pocket knife and carved the word

Greenland on it. The next time Rouse and I snuck down to the river I nailed it to a tall water oak and declared the site our Greenland.

Rouse and I went to the river all year round, even during the cold months of winter, till the year of the storm. That middle January day got real cold, then the reports started coming in on television. We were in for the hardest freeze ever known in our part of Alabama. Grandmamma said it was a sign from God and the end was coming. She said she hoped it took the river first, freezing it solid till it broke into chunks and was hauled away, never to run along her land again. She spent the day watching the weather updates and praying that come next morning the river would be gone.

We spent a cold night huddled in front of the fireplace feeding wood to the fire. Come next morning the river was still there but old Rouse was gone. I found him frozen to the back porch. I didn't think it was possible for anyone to be so sad without crying but no tears came. I couldn't feel my heart beat. At that moment something broke inside my head. That's the only way I can explain it. Like dropping a fragile drinking glass and watching it shatter into splinters. I knelt next to him rubbing his head trying to warm him till Grandmamma opened the back door. She had a big pot of steaming water in her hands.

"Get up and get away from it." I stood a few feet next to Rouse's head as she emptied the hot water over him.

"Take it and throw it out in the woods. The chain too. Far in the woods so come spring and it thaws I won't be smelling it."

I threw the chain in the woods but not my friend Rouse. I took him to our Greenland. The shallows of the river were frozen but the middle waters were still rushing. I held him at the river's edge not feeling the cold. Then placed him on the icy shallow and pushed him with a broken limb of the water oak. He slid easily till the rushing water picked him up swirling around him then carrying him downstream and out of sight.

I don't remember not eating for days. Didn't feel hunger, pain, cold or sadness. That January ice storm had taught me a new lesson. I learned to hate. Grandmamma was happy, went about her cleaning, praying and singing while she cooked. I watched and hated her movements and the sound of her voice. I was a sinner.

I missed Rouse. When I went to the river I talked with him and tossed his share of picnic buttered bread and honey in the river, watching it rush downstream. I walked along the bank hoping to find him in the nice place I thought the river had taken Grandmamma's husband and son. I came to an old bridge and crawled out on it on hands and knees looking down at the rushing water but didn't find Rouse.

Those days Mama was gone more than home. Grandmamma was tired of it and told Mama next time she took off to take me with her. Said she wanted me out from under foot and needed some peace for a change. I was nine years old and a week away from starting the fourth grade when Mama tossed me a sack and told me to pack. There was a different car waiting at the end of the lane. Mama pulling me along, giving instructions as to keeping quiet and out of her and her new friend's way. I got in the backseat and focused on the back of his head. He was a big man with thinning black hair that he tried to comb to cover his white scalp. The only time he spoke he asked Mama why she was bringing a kid along. Mama told him she didn't have no choice.

The man drove us into town and parked on a back street; then we walked around the corner to a drugstore. Mama told me to leave my sack of clothes in the car and handed me a five-dollar bill.

"Go in the drugstore, Little Bill, and wait for me at the soda fountain. I'll be next door in the big tall building and I'll come back for you in a little while. Get yourself a comic book, ice cream or a soda with the money I gave you."

I did as Mama said, sitting at the counter, looking at my comic and drinking sodas till my money ran out. The man behind the counter kept coming back and asking if I needed anything else, but I said no, that I didn't have any more money. He let me sit there till dark and it was time to close the store. He asked me where my mama was and I told him she was in the big tall building next door and she'd be back to get me anytime now. The man got a funny look on his face and then told me to wait there, said he'd go next door to the hotel and see if he could find my mama. It seemed like he was gone a long time before I heard loud sirens and saw lots of lights. Police cars were all along the street with men jumping out of them running along the sidewalk.

The man from behind the counter came back later, his face red, and with him was a policeman. The policeman sat down next to me, looking straight ahead, and then turned to me.

"What's your name, boy?"

"Little Bill."

"Little Bill, did you and your mama come to town by yourself?"

"No sir."

"Who brought you to town?"

"A man."

"You know this man, Little Bill?"

"No sir."

"Can you tell me what he looks like?"

"Big. Thin hair and a white scalp."

"Did he bring you and your mama here in a car?"

"Yes sir. Parked on the back street and we walked here."

"Can you tell me what his car looked like?"

"No sir."

"I want you to come with me, Little Bill. We think we found your mama."

He took me to the tall building next door and up the stairs to a long hallway. There were people standing all along the hall looking at me like they were sad. We stopped in front of a door that had the number twelve on it. The policeman squatted down and took me by the hand.

"Little Bill, I don't want you to be afraid. Can you go in this room with me and tell me if this is your mama?"

"Yes sir."

We went in with another policeman. The room was dimly lit and smelled funny. They walked me to the edge of the bed and Mama was there. She didn't have no clothes on, and one of her stockings was stuffed in her mouth, the other wrapped around her neck like a winter scarf. Her eyes were open but they didn't have no color or life to them. Looked like old Rouse's eyes when I found him froze to the porch.

"Is this your mama?"

"Yes sir."

They took me back to the hall and wanted to know where I lived before the man brought us to town. I told them in the big old house down on the banks of the river with grandmamma. The younger policeman called the other to the side.

"I think I know where the boy lives. The old Raines house. Other than going to church his grandmamma Bessie lives out there like a hermit. She's been that way ever since she lost her husband and son to the river. I went to school with her son, used to go out there and target shoot with him. They never found his body or her husband's. That woman in there has to be her daughter, called Judy or Judith. I'd nearly forgot she had a daughter because over the years nobody saw much of her because she was always up and taking off for long spells of time. I didn't even know she had a child. I'll take the boy home.

He's all the old woman's got now. I dread breaking the news to her that she's lost her daughter, but it may be easier if someone she might remember was the one to tell her."

When the policeman told Grandmamma she fell right down on the porch pulling her hair and screaming, "Judith! Judith!" He helped her inside and up the stairs to her room, Grandmamma screaming and fighting him all the way. The screaming didn't stop till the next morning when the policeman knocked on the door with Mama's small leather bag of personal belongings. Grandmamma stood there holding it, a look on her face like somebody had handed her a poisonous snake. Then she turned and went back upstairs without a word to the policeman. For the next two hours she played the same hymns on her phonograph over and over. At noon she came downstairs with Mama's leather bag and called me out to the kitchen.

"Little Bill, God has told me that you brought sin to my Judith. Sin that killed her. You were born a sinner and that's all you'll ever be. I told you that you should be good and free of evil but you never listened. So now you have to suffer your redemption and your mama's redemption. God said you need to eat the sins of your mama. Take off your clothes."

She took the dress and pair of high heels Mama had worn to town out of the bag and tossed them to me. I put them on, afraid to do anything else. Then she pulled out a tube of red lipstick and roughly coated my mouth with it in the shape of a heart.

"Now I'm going back upstairs. I want you to go outside and walk around this house till my hymns stop playing. I'll be watching you from every window, and so help me in the name of God if you stop before the hymns stop you will suffer more than redemption."

"But Grandmamma, I can't walk in these shoes."

She pushed me to the floor, walked to the kitchen drawer and pulled out a roll of black tape wrapping it around and around the shoes and my feet and legs.

"Get out of here and start walking."

The hymns played and I walked. In two hours I could feel the blisters coming with every step. Each time I slowed or stopped from the pain Grandmamma would yell from the window, "Walk! Eat your mama's sins!"

# # #

It was dusk when a young girl ran up alongside me.

"Hey! What's ya name?"

"Little Bill."

"My name's Katie. That shore is a purty dress ya wearin. I like them red high heels too. I always wanted a pair a purty red high-heeled shoes."

"They're no fun. Hurting my feet something awful."

"Then why ya out here walkin in em?"

"My grandmamma said I was a sinner and I got to do this to get free of sin and evil."

"She did, huh? Well, I bet I could help ya walk in them shoes. They look just the right size for me. Yep, wouldn't bother me none to walk in a pair a purty red high heels like them."

# # #

I felt a hard slap across my cheek and Grandmamma was standing there in the backyard with me. The sun was out and I had no idea what time it was.

"What is wrong with you, boy?" I called you in last night at ten o'clock and here you are still out here walking seven o'clock next morning. You trying to make a fool out of me and God? Get in the house!"

I didn't remember nothing about walking the day before and all night. Last thing I remembered was Katie talking and walking alongside me. When I took the black tape and high heels off, my feet were swollen and raw as hamburger, but funny thing was they didn't hurt at all.

"How are you going to start school next week with your feet swollen up like logs? How am I going to explain why you're not in school this time?"

I didn't say nothing, just went to bed. The first day of school I walked down the lane and got on the bus. I didn't feel no pain nor anything else. I just wanted to get out of that house and away from Grandmamma. If Mama was buried I didn't know nothing about it. That didn't make any difference either because I really didn't ever truly know Mama. To this day I don't know where they put her. Grandmamma never mentioned her by name again, just referred to her as "your mama" when she made me suffer my redemption. I was a sinner and needed a lot of redeeming grace.

When I was twelve, Grandmamma filled the tub with ice cold water after I refused to kneel with her in prayer. She made me strip down and sit in the icy water while scrubbing me down with sandpaper to wash away the sin. I didn't feel nothing but hate. Then I realized I was out of the tub and she was sitting in the corner with her hands held up in front of her face crying and praying.

"God help me! God help me! The devil is in my house!"

I reached out to help her to her feet but she cringed and screamed louder.

"Don't you touch me, devil! God, deliver me from this evil!"

She crawled on her hands and knees to her room and locked the door. The hymns played all night and next morning there was a mark on her right cheek. I guess I hit her but I don't remember.

I heard her talking on the phone in low tones with her pastor that afternoon. "I need prayers. The devil has taken Little Bill. Last night he knocked me to the floor. When I called him the devil he stood over me and didn't even look like himself. His face was different. For a moment I thought he might kill me. He told me his name was not Little Bill. Said his name was Joe! Send me prayers, Pastor, that I may cast this devil out of him."

I was convinced Grandmamma had finally lost her mind. She filled the house up with crosses, one over every door and window, and lined the walls of her bedroom with them. I stayed out of her way and she stayed out of mine. We didn't talk or even take our meals together, just existed like two prisoners in that cold, damp house. It went on like that till my second year of high school. The river was still my escape, my favorite place, and I went there daily, but I made a few friends in high school and started spending a lot of time with them. We would sneak into bars for beers and games of darts. Then one night they say I jumped a man for bumping into me and spilling my beer and I beat him badly. My friends said when they pulled me off him I tried to fight them too, saying, "Leave me alone or I'll kick your ass too! My name is Joe!"

There was that name Joe again and me with no memory of what happened at the bar. I feared I was losing my mind right along with Grandmamma. There were other reasons I was afraid. There were days when I woke up wearing Mama's dress and high heels, and sometimes I found scraps of the dress fabric snagged in the thorns of the wild blackberry bushes down by the river. I knew Katie had come back too along with Joe. I was scared and beginning to think maybe Grandmamma was right about the devil taking me. So I told her I was a sinner and asked if I could pray with her. She said no, that I could not be saved, and then said, "Speak to me never again, devil!"

I left the house for a long walk and two days later my friends called me aside and told me I had showed up at school the day before wearing a dirty suit, dress shirt and tie, calling myself Preacher Abbott. They said I stopped kids in the hall and preached to them till the principal sent me home for the day. My friends thought I'd gone nuts and they didn't want me hanging around them anymore. That afternoon when I got home from school I searched my room and found the dirty suit, shirt and tie folded neatly in Mama's leather bag with her dress, lipstick and red high heels.

I never went back to school. Didn't seem to be any point in it. I thought about getting a job but town was too many miles to walk to and my head was always too full of voices, making it impossible to concentrate or remember what I'd done or hadn't done. I couldn't even keep up with what day it was. Seemed like I was constantly losing time.

I guess it was a year maybe two later when one night the hymns stopped playing but the scratch of the phonograph needle kept up for an hour so I went upstairs to check on Grandmamma. She was in her bed covered with crosses, arms folded across her chest and her eyes closed.

They took her away the next morning. The pastor came that very same afternoon and told me Grandmamma had left the house, all its contents and all the land to the church. He said they'd give me a week to find some other place to live. That's how he said it, just short and simple. After he left I looked around at all those crosses hanging everywhere and thought Grandmamma and God had given me my final redemption punishment. They were putting me out in the cold just like old Rouse. I built a fire in the backyard then went through the house and collected every one of those crosses, burning them along with Grandmamma's phonograph, records, her clothes and even her Bible. I didn't want another sinner to come and live in the house and suffer the same redemption I had.

I woke up in Greenland the next morning, my clothes muddy and damp from the morning dew. When I reached the house there was nothing left but a pile of ashes and a few metal parts of the phonograph in the backyard. For a moment I was afraid to go inside knowing what I'd done would get me in trouble, but then I remembered Grandmamma was gone and couldn't hurt me anymore.

The next four days came and went, blurring in and out, the voices inside my head screaming. I'd wake to find the kitchen table set with four plates, the food half eaten, dried and beginning to spoil. The sixth day I sat in the living room knowing I had no place to go. My head hurt so bad it was hard to focus my eyes, the room waving, going up and down like a wild carnival ride. I closed my eyes and tried to think back. I couldn't understand what I'd done to become an evil sinner and to suffer redemption punishment all my life.

# # #

"I'm scared, Little Bill. We don't have but one more day to live here. Where we gonna go?"

"I don't know, Katie."

"It's all her fault. You should have killed the crazy old bitch the first time she laid hands on you. Good thing she went on and died or I would have killed her for you!"

"Shut up, Joe! Ya scare me when ya talk mean like that."

"I scare you? What are you going to do, Katie girl? You don't know nothing about what's going on. Just a scared little girl. So you shut up!"

"Both of you shut up! I can't think! My head hurts so badly!"

"The Lord our God will take care of us. He has a place prepared for all of us. Let us kneel and pray for the answer."

"You can shut your mouth too, Preacher Abbott, right along with Katie. It was that old bitch and God that got us here. What are you going to do? Pray us into another home or maybe a hotel room?"

"Please be quiet! I can't think when you all talk at once! I can't think! I can't think! I can't think!"

"Little Bill, I like this house. I don't wanna go!"

"We have to go, Katie. This isn't my home anymore."

"We could hide. I'm good at hide-and-seek. I could hide all of us and they'd never find us."

"God will show us the way. Kneel with me and pray!"

"Now I've heard it all. This dumb-ass preacher and dim-witted little girl gonna solve all our problems with a prayer and a game of hide-and-seek. Are you laughing with me, Little Bill?"

"Don't be mean to Katie or the preacher, Joe. It's terrible to be mean and hurt people."

"Didn't bother you when I knocked that old bitch down and saved you from cold water and sandpaper, and didn't bother you when I kicked that jerk's ass in the bar."

"I never asked any of you to do anything for me. Why can't you leave me be? I wish you'd all go away!"

"Don't be mad at us, Little Bill. Don't wish us away. We came cause ya needed us. We'll do what ya say. Where ya wanna go?"

"Down to the river, Katie."

"What we gonna do down at the river? We can't live there, can we? Why ya wanna go to the river?"

"The river is my favorite place. I always go to the river when I'm troubled."

"Okay, we'll all go down to the river. Right, guys?"

"I guess. I'm totally bored with all this yakking."

"We could kneel and pray when we get there."

"I told you to shut up, Preacher. There won't be any praying tonight."

# # #

"How much farther, Little Bill? I'm tired and cold."

"We're almost there, Katie. The bridge is just a little ways down the path."

"Will ya carry me, Joe?"

"Silly girl, come here and climb up on my back. Don't ever say I never did nothing for you."

"I'll sing us a nice hymn while we walk. 'Amazing Grace' is my favorite."

"Shut up, Preacher, and save your breath for walking."

"Stop arguing. We're here. Be careful on the bridge, it's old and rickety."

"What we gonna do now?"

"We're going to jump into the river, Katie, and let it take us to a nice place. Same place it took old Rouse."

"All of us?"

"Yes, Katie. All of us."

"The water looks cold and black. It don't look like no nice place."

"The water will take us to the nice place. Trust me."

"Are ya scared, Little Bill?"

"No, Katie."

"I'm real scared, Little Bill."

"Hell, I'm not scared. Anyplace would be better than where we been through the years. I'm with you, Little Bill. How about you, preacher man? You got the balls for this?"

"To take one's own life is a sin and you can't get into heaven! We'll be doomed to an eternity in hell!"

"Don't sound much different than where you, me, Little Bill and Katie have been all our life."

"Don't be afraid, Katie. I'll hold your hand and so will Joe. And Preacher Abbott will hold mine."

"Can I say a prayer now, Little Bill? The rest of you don't have to pray with me if you don't want to."

"Yes, say a prayer for all of us."

"Our Father, which art in heaven, hallowed be thy Name. Thy Kingdom come. Thy will be done in earth, as it is in heaven. Give us this day our daily bread. And forgive us our trespasses, as we forgive them that trespass against us. And lead us not into temptation, but deliver us from evil. For thine is the Kingdom, the Power, and the Glory, for ever and ever. Amen."

"Amen."

"Amen."

"Amen."

"Take my hand, Katie. Joe, take Katie's hand. Preacher Abbot, take my hand."

"But Little Bill, I'm so scared. What if I get lost? Ya hold my hand tight? Ya won't let go?"

"I'll hold tight. You won't get lost. We'll all be together. Good night, Katie. Time to go."

# # #

"Sister Ellen, if you don't mind, start packing up the stuff downstairs and I'll go upstairs to clean out the boy's room. No telling what I'll find there. It may be unpleasant."

"I heard they found his body washed up in the shallows three miles past the old bridge. It's all so sad, Pastor. Such a young man. Did you know him?"

"Not really. I knew his grandmamma well. She was a member of my church and a good Christian woman. She spent her whole life taking care of that wild daughter of hers and the boy, who obviously had problems. Miss Bessie was afraid of him along toward the end. She called me many times asking for prayers. I can't help but think it was the stress of it all that took her to an early grave. It always saddens me to lose a faithful parishioner but especially one who has lived her life loving and nurturing her family, God and her church."

"Does anyone know why he took his life? Did he leave a note?"

"I guess you could say he left a note but not on paper. It was odd. There was definitely something wrong with him. The closest thing to a note we found was a long two-pronged fork embedded in the kitchen table, and written in the dust on the table top were the words, 'Thanks for nothing Grandmamma.'"

Author's Note

At completion I shared this story with a fellow writer. In part of his critique he wrote: "I'm impressed that your narrator is a ghost. How do you make that work so well? It doesn't seem like it should be possible."

It may sound odd, but I did not realize I had written Little Bill's story that way. His story has stayed with me and he has haunted me for many years. I have felt guilt, that at the time, I had little knowledge of multiple personalities and did not recognize how desperately ill he was.

He was very articulate in telling me about his life, but at the same time, he told his story, as if he were telling someone else's. He never reflected anger toward his abusers. It was not till his death and the note written in dust, that I knew how horrific his life must have been.

I never met Joe, the angry personality, but heard of the episode at the bar and even then found it difficult to believe that it was my friend Bill. Since his death, he has come to me in dreams and at times I have felt his presence, like a whisper in my ear, "Tell my story."

Now that his story is written, the dreams have stopped, his presence absent. I truly think he is content and has taken his leave. Godspeed, Little Bill.

Jan Fink

VI.

The Driving Lesson

"**Y**ou okay?"

"I don't know. I think my nose might be broken. What happened?"

"She ran us into a tree. Now she's sitting up there, not moving or saying nothing."

Dylan pulled his T-shirt up to his nose to stop the blood that was running down his upper lip, into his mouth and down his chin, then leaned over the front seat and touched his aunt's shoulder.

"Aunt Gatha."

A murder of crows at the edge of the cornfield took flight, breaking the silence with loud caws that made Dylan jump and fall back into the backseat.

"See, I told you, she aint said nothing since we hit the tree."

"Jeez Pauley, how long was I knocked out?"

"Long enough to scare me, brother."

"Just shut up Pauley. This was all your idea. Now look what a mess."

"Wait a minute. When I said Dylan let's go over and get Aunt Gatha and teach her to drive I don't recall you hanging back or saying anything like, Oh no, Pauley, let's not do that. You're in this same as me, and it's your fault same as my mine. We gotta think this through."

They sat quietly, Dylan with his head back and shirt stuffed up his nostrils while Pauley tapped his nails on the armrest. Pauley had bought the '68 Chevy Impala at an auction a year earlier so he and Dylan would have their own way of getting about. The only other automobile on the farm was their Granddaddy's truck and Granddaddy had made it clear from the start that he wouldn't share his truck with his wild-ass grandsons. He never referred to the boys by name. It was always those "wild-ass boys did this" or "those crazy wild-ass boys did that."

Granddaddy was on the front porch the day Pauley drove the car up to the house amid a cloud of dust and black smoke. The Chevy was already slinging oil from the twenty-mile trip home from the auction. When Pauley shut off the engine, got out and pointed with pride to the old car, Granddaddy remained seated, not even bothering to come out and give it a look over. He just shouted over his shoulder.

"Grammy, come on out here and take a look at what this crazy wild-ass boy has done now!"

Granddaddy's words were going through Pauley's mind. Yeah, if Granddaddy was standing here right this minute, Pauley was sure he'd be saying, "Take a look at what this crazy, wild-ass boy has done now." That's what Granddaddy would say and he'd be right this time, but Pauley wasn't about to admit that to Dylan. He couldn't let on that any of this had him the least bit worried. He was the oldest and Dylan looked up to him.

"Come on Dylan, let's check out the damage."

The front end of the Chevy was wrapped around the base of a large pine. The car's grill looked like it was holding the tree trunk between a thumb and forefinger to keep it from crashing to the ground. Steam and smoke were rising from under the hood, the radiator hissing like a snake about to strike. Pauley and Dylan climbed onto the hood and sat facing the windshield.

"Damn, Pauley. We killed her."

Aunt Gatha was behind the steering wheel smiling, her head pressed forward, flush with the windshield. There wasn't a speck of blood on her, just a small crack in the glass where her head made impact. The crack in the glass had run a path up and above her head, making a complete circle. Dylan thought she looked as if she'd already got her halo. Maybe that was why she was smiling; she was up in heaven with her halo. Gatha *was* smiling. Her hands were still gripping the steering wheel, her eyes wide open and the biggest smile you ever did see spread across her face.

"Pauley, would you look at how she's smiling? It's spooky. You think she's not dead? Maybe we ought to try and get her to a doctor?" Pauley leaned a little closer to the windshield and looked into Gatha's eyes.

"She's dead all right. Come on Dylan, don't go all weird on me. There's nothing spooky about her smiling. She was having fun. For a short while she was driving and laughing and loving it. I say we showed her a real good time."

"Well Pauley, I say we killed her."

"We did nothing of the sort. How were we to know she'd get behind the wheel, slam her big fat foot down on the gas pedal, tear across the cornfield like a loose pig and run into the only tree in sight? You know what confuses me? Think about it, Dylan. One tree in the middle of acres of land and Aunt Gatha takes a bead on it and closes in like a guided missile. It doesn't make sense. No sense at all unless she was trying to kill herself. You know, this gives me an idea. What say, we tell Granddaddy and the rest of the family that we heard a crash, ran down here and found Aunt Gatha smashed behind the steering wheel of the car?"

"Pauley, stop and think. Everybody knows Aunt Gatha can't drive. Do you really think they're going to believe she walked up to the house and said, 'Hey Pauley, you mind if I borrow your car? I got up this morning and it's such a fine day I was thinking of going for a drive.' It won't work. You got to come up with something better than that, brother."

Pauley sat cross legged on the hood of the car, still watching Aunt Gatha through the windshield, as if maybe she would stick her head out the car window and make a suggestion.

"You got any ideas, Dylan?"

"No, I don't. I only know come a week from now when Granddaddy and Grammy get back from the farmers convention we better damn sure have some idea of what to tell them. Damn you, you're always getting me in trouble. You've pulled some good ones, but this… this, Pauley, this is bad!"

Dylan looked back at his aunt, hoping for signs of life. She was still holding the steering wheel and smiling like the Cheshire cat.

# # #

Dylan didn't know why he'd never been able to learn his lesson and say no when it came to getting into trouble with Pauley. Up to now it had been little trouble, but this time it was big trouble. In his heart Dylan knew he'd never had a whole lot of choice. Pauley was his big brother and after their dad up and left Dylan was all he had other than his mom, Sue. Sue had struggled along for six months after their dad deserted them; never making ends meet till she realized her husband wasn't coming back. When the rent came due the seventh month she picked up Dylan and Pauley, left Atlanta and moved in with her parents on their farm in rural Tennessee.

When Pauley first laid eyes on their new home, he'd said it was so far out in the sticks there was nothing *but* sticks. Dylan agreed with Pauley, compared to Atlanta, there was nothing nearby except a church five miles to the east and Aunt Gatha and Uncle George's place a mile to the south. As for the church,

Dylan couldn't understand how or why it kept its doors open. There was only the minister, Preacher Fuller, and a congregation of four: Granddaddy, Grammy, Aunt Gatha and Uncle George. From their first day on the farm Grammy had tried to get Pauley, Dylan and Sue interested in joining the church, but it took just one visit to stop short that ambition. That Sunday morning Grammy was so proud to be bringing possible converts into Preacher Fuller's fold.

"Praise God, Preacher Fuller, the Lord has led my loved ones to the door of this church."

Granddaddy, Grammy, Aunt Gatha and Uncle George took seats on the front pew. Pauley giggled then joined Dylan and Sue on the back pew near the door, then settled in with a look of boredom, took out his pocket knife and began cleaning the dirt from under his fingernails. Preacher Fuller began his sermon. Two hours into talk of good and evil Sue could stand it no more. She pulled a bottle of cherry red nail polish from her purse and began painting her nails. The chemical smell of the nail enamel quickly filled the little church.

Uncle George had lost his sight in a coal mining accident ten years back, but his sense of smell was still strong. He tilted his head back toward the headrest of his pew and stiffed the air. His blank eyes rolled back in his head and he jumped to his feet.

"Praise God, Preacher Fuller, do you smell that? I do believe the spirit of God has entered this church. Praise God! Praise God!"

Uncle George began to sway back and forth shouting, "Praise God! Praise God!" Aunt Gatha joined him, clapping her hands and stamping her feet each time he shouted. Preacher Fuller thought he'd brought the Holy Spirit into the church single-handed with his sermon. He pounded the pulpit, raised his arms to the heavens and began singing Amazing Grace. Granddaddy was on his feet, Grammy alongside him, clapping and singing along with Preacher Fuller. It was in the midst of praise when Pauley stood and walked to the pulpit.

"Praise God indeed! I feel the spirit. It wants me to testify. Praise God, I'm in the sticks, so far out in the sticks there aint nothing but sticks. I sit on sticks. I sleep on sticks. I brush my teeth with sticks. I eat sticks; I use sticks to eat my sticks. Yes, Praise God, I wipe my butt with sticks!"

Grammy swooned; gripping the back of her pew and at that moment saw Sue applying her second coat of nail polish. She righted herself and turned back to Pauley, who was still praising God and sticks. She walked over, grabbed him by his left ear and dragged him to the back pew. She picked up Sue on her way out of the church, grabbing her right ear, making her smear the polish on her left pinky nail. She marched them both into the church yard, holding to their ears and cursing them to hell and forever damnation. That was the beginning and end of Dylan, Pauley and Sue's religious period.

Grammy had Preacher Fuller over for dinner each Sunday after services. Only one coffee, a rich, dark blend would do to serve with peach cobbler after the meal and Grammy had it delivered every Sunday morning. Sue's job was to watch for the delivery man and call the grocer if by chance the coffee didn't arrive. Sue began going out to meet the delivery man at his truck instead of waiting for him to knock. Dylan had watched her. She'd take the coffee and then stand, looking up at him, giggling and talking, her hands with cherry red nails propped on her hips. Six months later Grammy returned from church, tied on her apron and went to the kitchen to start Sunday dinner. There on the kitchen counter was her coffee order, with a note taped to the top of the can.

Here is your precious coffee.

Hell and Forever Damnation to You Too.

Goodbye.

The note was signed, "Your Daughter Sue," in cherry red nail polish. Dylan and Pauley didn't know where their mom was now, but wherever it was they were sure she was in the company of the delivery man. From that day on, Grammy and

Granddaddy wouldn't allow coffee in the house. They never mentioned Sue—just went on about the farm work as if they didn't have a daughter. They did the Christian thing and let the boys stay on, but it was obvious that they barely tolerated them. Now Dylan had only Pauley and Pauley had only Dylan. No matter what happened, good or bad, they were in this together.

# # #

Dylan jumped down from the hood of the car. When his feet hit the ground it felt like someone had thrown a cinder block in his face. His head was throbbing and his nose was bleeding again, so he tilted his head back and pulled his already bloody shirt to his nose to stay the flow. He leaned against the front of the car to clear his head and think of something that would get him and his brother out of trouble.

"Pauley."

"Yeah."

"This is just a thought. I aint saying it would work, but what if we could get Aunt Gatha back to her house and maybe sit her up in a chair or something? When they find her they'll think she died of natural causes. Damn, I bet she weighs nearly four hundred pounds. They might think her heart couldn't take all that weight she was carrying around and it just gave up."

"Dylan, you're a genius! You may be quiet most of the time, but I always knew in my heart we had the same conniving blood coursing through our veins. You just proved it brother."

Pauley stood up and leaped from the hood of the car. He pulled a dried corn stalk from the ground, pressed the leaves to his chest and danced around the Chevy.

"It'll work brother! Take Aunt Gatha home. Genius! I think that's exactly where she'd like to be right now. Uncle George was asleep when we picked her up this morning. Hell, Uncle George can't see his hand in front of his face. If we get her back to the house he won't even know she's dead till he goes to the supper table and there aint no food. We'll take Aunt Gatha and prop her up in a chair on the porch and come dinner time he'll go looking for her and bam! He finds her on the porch passed away."

"You're forgetting one thing, Pauley. This car aint going nowhere and you and I sure can't pick up all four hundred pounds of her and carry her all the way to her porch."

Pauley tossed his corn stalk dance partner aside and sat down on the nearest corn row. He picked up dirt clods and threw them at the tires of the Chevy. They pinged against the hubcaps, scattering into dust particles that puffed in the breeze, then settled on the windshield and Gatha's halo.

"I got it Dylan! We'll use Granddaddy's potato slide. All we have to do is harness up the mule, pull the slide out here, push Aunt Gatha out onto it and let the mule haul her right over to her front porch."

Pauley volunteered to fetch the mule and slide while Dylan stayed with the car. His nose had stopped bleeding, but now it felt like it was the size of a naval orange. When his brother was out of sight he looked back through the windshield. "Aunt Gatha, I sure am sorry about all this. We were just looking for something to do. Pauley thought teaching you to drive would be a fun way to pass the morning. We didn't expect it to turn out like this. We sure didn't mean to kill you."

Dylan could see Pauley leading the mule across the field, the slide following behind. A week earlier he and his brother had walked alongside the rig digging potatoes and tossing them onto the slide as Granddaddy guided the mule up and down the rows of the field. Now they were going to toss poor old dead Aunt Gatha onto the slide. Pauley positioned the slide next to the driver's side, opened the car door and then stood there with his hands in his pockets.

"Dylan, you reckon she feels all cold and clammy like they say dead bodies do?"

"I don't know. Pull her out and see."

"I sure hate to touch her. Kind of seems like violating the dead."

"Pauley, we've already done all the violating can be done. We killed her!"

"Jeez, Dylan! Will you please stop saying we killed her? Come on, let's get this over with."

Pauley reached in and pried Gatha's hands from the steering wheel and leaned her back against the seat. Both boys took an arm and attempted to pull her out onto the slide. They tugged at her arms, but she barely budged. It was as if she was made of soft stretch plastic that snapped back in place each time the boys pulled, their effort moving her no more than an inch. Pauley went around to the passenger side, climbed in, closed the door and braced his back against it. He held onto the dashboard and pushed Gatha with his feet while Dylan pulled. She gave suddenly, popping out of the car like a pimento squeezed from an olive. Dylan was kneeling on the slide and didn't have time to get out of the way. Gatha landed face up, smiling at the sun with Dylan wedged underneath her. The mule came close to bolting. It stood trembling, nostrils flared, ears straight up, undecided about running and taking the slide, Dylan and Gatha with him.

"Get her off! Pauley, get her off of me!"

Pauley scrambled from the car, grabbed Dylan beneath his armpits and pulled him from under Gatha. Dylan jumped to his feet and began turning in short circles, running his hands up and down his clothing. He'd heard of this state of mind and knew he was having an attack of heebee jeebees, but he was helpless to stop it till it had run its course. After a few minutes the attack subsided, but in the pit of his stomach he felt that the heebee jeebees were going to come back any minute and tear into him.

"You all right? Did she crush you?"

"No, she didn't crush me, just scared me. I didn't want that dead body lying on me one more second."

They looked down at Gatha. Pauley shook his head. "Just look at her. Not a clue as to all the trouble she's causing. She's still smiling, happy as can be."

The boys led the mule, pulling the slide and Gatha the mile to her house. They paused when they reached the yard. Uncle George wasn't on the porch, he was still napping, their luck was holding. They positioned the slide at the porch steps, then as quietly as possible rolled Gatha off the slide, pushing her foot by foot up the steps onto the porch. During the process Uncle George's old Blue Tick hound came around the corner of the house. He didn't bark, just stood there in the yard, watching with mild curiosity. Pauley and Dylan agreed that the rolling and pushing part had been fairly easy, but getting Gatha in her porch rocker was going to be almost impossible.

Gatha hadn't always been obese. Years back Uncle George had splurged on her birthday and given her a large box of chocolates and she fell in love with the stuff. Chocolate came to mean so much to her that George started sending Grammy to town each year after Halloween to buy up all the discounted candy she could find. They kept it stored year round in an old deep freeze on the back porch. That way Gatha could have chocolate any time she pleased, and she pleased all the time. Every year she gained more weight and soon it was impossible for her to sit in regular chairs. Grammy found a love seat rocker built for two at the hardware and had it sent down to Gatha so she could sit on the porch during cool evenings.

Pauley and Dylan managed to get Gatha into her rocker by tipping it forward, pushing her in, and then righting the rocker. The wood and nails groaned and cracked, but held till they got Gatha and the rocker upright. They placed her hands on the arms of the rocker and stood back to inspect their work.

"See," Pauley said, "We got her home safely Dylan, and look at her sitting in her rocker smiling. I think she's even happier now."

Dylan couldn't bring himself to respond. They decided to tell Granddaddy they'd wrecked the car while joy riding in the field. Granddaddy wouldn't have a problem believing that was possible, just those crazy wild-ass boys at it again. They took the mule and slide back to the barn, went home and waited.

# # #

George felt for the cane he kept beside his bed. His fingers grasped it, he stood and tapped his way down the hall, through the front door and onto the porch.

"Gatha, honey, ya out here? I thought I heard a bumping noise earlier. Ya didn't fall did ya baby?" When Gatha didn't answer he reached out in the direction of the rocker and touched her shoulder.

"Why didn't ya answer me? Ya okay? Oh, I see. Ya in one of ya quiet moods, huh. Well, I'll just sit over here and let ya get over ya spell. I know how ya are when ya want to be left alone." George sat down in his rocker at the opposite side of the porch and breathed in the evening air, humming and tapping his cane for rhythm. George sat on the porch with Gatha till late that night, then excused himself and went back to bed.

# # #

Pauley and Dylan had slept in their clothes, certain their Uncle George would come in the middle of the night, his cane tapping the front door and screaming, but it was morning and he hadn't come. They ate a light breakfast, waited till noon then decided to walk down the lane and take a look. As soon as the house came into view they could see Gatha in the rocker just as they'd left her. When they entered the yard the old Blue Tick rounded the corner of the house, and this time he did bark. They heard the tapping of George's cane coming down the entrance hall and then stop at the screen door.

"Pauley, Dylan, is that ya boys?" The boys stood silent, punching one another till Pauley spoke up.

"Yes sir, it's us Uncle George."

"Well, it's nice of ya boys to come and check on us, but ya Aunt Gatha is in one her not so social moods. Depressed I guess. We're running low on her sweets and the Halloween sale is a long ways off. Bless her heart, won't say a word. She stayed out here on the porch the night long, didn't make me a bite of supper and this morning I had to get my own cereal."

Pauley gave Dylan a look of amazement. "We'll go on back home and visit you later when Aunt Gatha is in a better mood."

"No, no. Sit and stay awhile. Ya walked all the way down here and besides, maybe ya boys can cheer her up. Come on in to the porch."

Pauley and Dylan took seats in the straight back chairs at the edge of the porch. They rolled their eyes at one another in disbelief. Pauley gave Dylan a wink, then said, "Aunt Gatha, how you feeling? You okay this morning?" George cocked his head in Gatha's direction. There was only silence. "See there," George said, "Just like I told ya, she won't say a word."

"Oh, but she nodded her head, Uncle George. She nodded her head yes, that she's feeling okay."

"Well good! Now we're making progress. Dylan, why don't ya run back there to the deep freeze and fetch ya Aunt some candies. Her favorite is the chocolate ones with peanut butter centers. I think there's still a five pound bag a them left. That'll make her real happy and maybe get her talking again."

Dylan went to the deep freeze and rifled through the bags of candy till he found the chocolates with peanut butter centers. He carried the bag back to the porch and placed it in his aunt's lap. God, he thought, I'm bringing candy to a dead woman. For an instant he felt the heebee jeebees sneaking up on him.

The boys sat for an hour as George talked of crops and weather, stopping from time to time to ask the boys if Gatha was eating her candy. Each time they'd say yes. The candy was being eaten, but not by Gatha. The Blue Tick was feasting. The hound acted as if he knew the situation. He'd look up at the boys from time to time and Dylan could swear the hound was smiling. He was sure that damn hound knew that blind Uncle George couldn't see him; Aunt Gatha was dead and the boys weren't going to raise a hand to him and chase him from the candy because he'd been right there when they rolled Gatha's dead body up the steps.

George could hear the candy wrappers rustling and chewing sounds. Even if his sweet Gatha wasn't talking, he was happy that at least she was eating her sweets. Pauley watched the hound and Uncle George and thought it was perfect for the hound, George, and perfect all around.

# # #

The morning of the third day, Pauley and Dylan didn't bother with breakfast. They sat at the kitchen table, wondering what to do next.

"Dylan, Uncle George is a lot stupider than I thought. His wife's been sitting out there on the porch going on the third day, not moving and not talking and he don't have a clue. All this would have been a lot easier if he had the least bit of smarts. Jeez, we could have already had her funeral and buried her before Granddaddy and Grammy got back."

"Obviously thanks to Uncle George, that's not going to happen. So what do we do now?"

"I guess we go check on them every day. If Uncle George doesn't catch on that his wife is dead before Granddaddy and Grammy get home we'll claim we never even visited them. Uncle George is close to being crazy anyway. We'll tell everybody he imagined our visits."

They had a quick glass of milk, then left to do their daily check. Gatha was still in her rocker smiling, but her color didn't look so good. The shape of her face had changed. It looked like one of those old witch masks kids wear for Trick or Treat, kind of white, blue and mottled but with a happy smile rather than an evil grin. There was also the smell, strong enough to make Dylan's stomach cramp and come close to losing his breakfast glass of milk. There were candy wrappers and smears of chocolate, caramel and peanut butter all over the porch floor. The Blue Tick lay at Gatha's feet and this time he growled as the boys came onto the porch. They waded through the candy wrappers and knocked on the screen door.

"That ya boys?'

"Yes sir. Thought we'd see how you're getting along."

"Good. Real good. Ya Aunt Gatha is fine too. She still aint talking to me. I can't imagine what I did to make her so mad. I been bringing her sweets to her ever evening, putting them in her lap and I can hear her enjoying them but she don't utter a word in my direction. This is the longest spell that woman has ever had. Maybe she misses Grammy. That's probably it. You know how close them two sisters are. I bet the minute Grammy gets back Gatha will be her old self again. In the meantime boys, if ya don't mind, check up under the porch for me. I've smelled an awful stink out here this morning. I'm afraid that old hound of mine has crawled up under this porch and died."

"Your old hound is fine. He's right here on the porch. This morning Dylan and I did see some vultures circling out there to the left of the house. It's probably a dead coon. We'll find it and bury it, right Dylan?"

Dylan stood gazing at what used to be his Aunt. Up close he realized she seemed to be sitting lower in the rocker and what looked like a smile from a distance was deceiving. The corners of her mouth were now turned down in a smile turned upside down. Pauley elbowed Dylan, waiting for a response.

"Yeah. We'll take care of that dead coon for you." The boys took three steps toward leaving the porch. The hound got up, growling. The fur on his back bristled and he bared his teeth. George opened the screen door and held out his cane.

"What has gotten into that hound? Ya boys take my cane and beat the hell out of him, growling at a family member that a way. I won't put up with it!" Dylan grabbed the cane and pushed it back. "That's okay Uncle George. He's old, we just startled him. He's not gonna bite us." George beat the cane on the porch floor. "He better not bite a one of ya. I may be blind but I can damn sure find a biting dog and beat hell out of it. Ya okay, Gatha baby? That hound didn't nip at ya did he?"

"She's okay! The hound didn't nip her Uncle George." That was enough for George; he closed the screen door and tapped his way down the hall, still cussing the hound.

It wasn't enough for Pauley and Dylan. Gatha was far from okay. That stupid old hound hadn't been content with the five-pound bags of candy George placed on Gatha's lap each evening. No, the Blue Tick hadn't nipped Gatha, he was eating her. The boys didn't realize this till the hound stood and growled at them. That's when they saw that her leg had been eaten away half way to her knee. Pauley took Dylan by the arm and pulled him in a slow run off the porch and down the lane. When they were out of sight of the porch, Gatha and the hound, he let go of Dylan's arm. Dylan fell to his knees, vomited and began to laugh. The effort of vomiting made his nose throb and a trickle of blood run down his upper lip. Dylan wiped it away with the back of his hand and laughed harder.

"Can you believe it, Pauley? Here we are worried about Granddaddy and Grammy coming home and finding Aunt Gatha and this hound is taking care of the problem for us! With his appetite by the end of the week there'll be nothing left but her bones buried in the backyard, a bunch of candy wrappers on the porch and Uncle George wondering where his sweet Gatha is. We'll tell him she ran off with the new delivery man. No, better yet, she ran off with a candy salesman. Don't you see, Pauley? That old hound's our friend. He's taking care of business for us!" Dylan rose while he talked and began running in circles, waving his arms uncontrollably. Heebee Jeebees. Pauley grabbed Dylan's shoulders and slapped him sharply across the face, sending pain to the top of Dylan's head and more blood running from his nose.

"You listen to me Dylan. That hound is not our friend. He's not going to take care of business for us. He's spoiling our plan. We have to go back and kill that damn hound. You hear me? The Blue Tick has got to go!"

"Okay Pauley, we kill the hound. Then what?"

"Then we're back to our original plan. Granddaddy and Grammy come home and find Aunt Gatha. Uncle George is declared crazy as a loon for not knowing she's been dead for days and we say, hey, we don't know nothing about it. Stick with me, brother. Let's take down the hound. See, one less problem."

"How we gonna take him down?"

"Come late tomorrow afternoon when Uncle George brings out the candy and puts it in Aunt Gatha's lap, we'll both be there in the yard watching till he goes back inside. You take the bag of candy and lead that damn hound out to the edge of the yard and I'll take it from there."

Dylan did as he was instructed. When Uncle George went back inside for his afternoon nap Dylan crept onto the porch. The hound stood ridge-backed and snarling as Dylan slowly picked up the bag of candy from Gatha's lap.

"Where you going with my candy?"

Dylan froze and looked about the porch and yard. No one there and no one at the screen door either. He reached into the bag of candy, took a step back and dropped a piece for the hound. The Blue Tick ate it wrapper and all, then growled.

"Don't give my candy to that hound. Chocolate will kill a hound. You don't want to kill your Uncle's hound do you?"

A gust of wind raced across the porch. Gatha's rocker creaked and moved slightly forward. Dylan took another step back and whispered viciously. "Pauley, stop it! If you're doing this, it aint funny. You keep messing with me and I'll go back home."

"Dylan? What's wrong with you boy? Don't you know your own Aunt's voice? By the way, where is Pauley? I'm feeling kinda poorly today, but when you see Pauley tell him that soon as I'm feeling better I'll be ready for another driving lesson. I sure had fun with you boys."

Dylan dropped the chocolates and ran into the yard, calling out to Pauley.

"I'm out here behind the house. Bring the hound back here."

"No, Pauley. I think she's alive!" Pauley came out of the shadows, looking behind Dylan and around the yard.

"Where's the hound?"

"You don't understand. She's still alive!"

"What the hell are you talking about?"

"Aunt Gatha. She, she, she just spoke to me. She wants another driving lesson."

"Brother, I'm starting to really worry about you. She can't talk to you. She's dead and rotting on the front porch. Are you going as crazy as Uncle George? Go back to the porch, take that bag of candy and lure that hound around here to me."

"No. Aunt Gatha said not give a hound chocolate. It'll kill him!"

"Dylan, what do you think we're here to do? Now calm down and get it together. I can't do this by myself. Remember brother, we're in this together. Turn around, go back to the porch and bring me the hound."

"Okay. I'll, I'll just not look at her."

"That's right, Dylan. Don't look at her."

Dylan teased the Blue Tick, dropping one candy at a time, leading him to the backyard. Pauley stood quietly, leaning against the house. Dylan emptied the bag of candy on the ground. The hound began to eat and as Pauley promised, he took it from there. The ax met the old hound's head with such force it sent the Blue Tick's nose smashing into the chocolates. Dylan didn't feel one way or the other about it, just stood staring down at the hound thinking it's over, at least this part is over. He picked up a chocolate near the hound's limp head, tossed it in his mouth and walked home. He left Pauley to deal with the Blue Tick; he didn't care what Pauley did with it. For all he cared Pauley could take the old hound back to the porch and prop him up, skull caved in, next to Aunt Gatha's cold, blue, half-eaten leg.

# # #

Granddaddy called that evening to say he and Grammy were leaving the Farmer's Convention early and would be home the next morning. Dylan tried to sleep but the events of the last week kept playing over and over in his mind. He wanted to get up and go down the lane to see if it was all real, but he knew it was real. He could still taste the chocolate that he'd picked up next to the Blue Tick's head. He lay awake rehearsing the plan Pauley had gone over with him earlier in the evening. He repeated his lines till long past midnight and sleep found him. He dreamt that he walked out to the cornfield to check on Pauley's car. Aunt Gatha and the Blue Tick were there holding hands and dancing around the Chevy. In the starlight he could see that the hound had a big smile on his face just like Aunt Gatha the day of the driving lesson. His mom Sue and the delivery man walked out of the shadows and joined Gatha and the hound. They all held hands and danced under the moon and stars. Then they stopped dancing and turned toward him, still smiling. Sue held her hand out for him to join them. Dylan woke covered in sweat, nauseated and frightened. The dream left him unable to sleep, so he lay awake the rest of the night waiting for the sun to come up and the sound of Granddaddy's truck.

# # #

They arrived at eight, the truck loaded with pamphlets, seed samples, vegetables, eggs and fresh butter. Pauley and Dylan offered to help with the unloading as Granddaddy watched them, suspicion in his eyes.

"You wild-ass boys feed my mule and checked on your Aunt Gatha and Uncle George while we been gone?"

"Ah, yes sir, we fed the mule but we aint seen Aunt Gatha and Uncle George. Me and Dylan had a little mishap this week. We took the Chevy down to the cornfield and I guess Dylan was driving too fast, hit that loose field dirt and ran us right into that big pine in the middle of the cornfield. Wrecked the Chevy real good! I'm so sore I can barely get around and Dylan got knocked into the windshield and thinks maybe his nose is broke. We've both stayed home, taking it easy and trying to get over it."

"Wrecked your car, did you? Well don't get any ideas about using my pickup, crazy wild ass-boys."

"No sir, we won't." Pauley lifted the basket of eggs from the truck bed and started toward the house.

"Wait Pauley. Give those to me. I'm going to take them down to Gatha and tell her about our trip. Put everything else in the house. I'll be back in a while and take a look at Dylan's nose to see if we need to get him to the doctor." Pauley and Dylan watched Grammy till she made the turn in the lane. They kept busy unloading the truck.

At the turn in the lane Grammy could see Gatha on the porch in her love seat rocker, then noticed an odd smell that hung heavy in the air. A breeze kicked up, blowing down the lane in her direction and intensifying the odor. It was strong enough to make her gag. She took a handkerchief from her apron pocket, held it to her nose and continued down the lane, mumbling.

"George has let their septic tank back up again. I can't believe he's let this happen three times this year. Forgive me Lord, but I do wish my sister hadn't married such a worthless man who never sees fit to take care of anything." When she reached the edge of the yard she could see her sister clearly. The basket slipped from her hand, falling at her feet. The eggs shattered, spraying egg whites and yellow yolks along the hem of her dress and apron.

"Oh God! Oh God! Oh, good God in heaven!" She turned, stumbling and screaming, trying to run back down the lane. Pauley and Dylan heard her screams first. Pauley took Dylan by the arm and shook him gently, then whispered, "Stick to the story." They called Granddaddy from the house as Grammy reached the yard and collapsed. She couldn't speak other than to scream "Oh, God." Granddaddy tried to help her to her feet but she refused to stand, her hands shaking and pointing down the lane. Granddaddy told the boys to stay with her, got in his truck and sped away.

# # #

The funeral was brief, casket closed. Preacher Fuller's sermon took no more than ten minutes. Pauley and Dylan sat on the back pew where their mom Sue had painted her nails and stirred up the Holy Spirit during their one and only time attending church. This time Pauley didn't go to the pulpit to testify; he sat with his head bowed and kept silent. After the burial, Grammy invited Preacher Fuller for dinner and prayer.

When the meal was done they all sat on the porch while Preacher Fuller led them in prayer. Uncle George was quiet. He hadn't eaten or spoken a word since Granddaddy took him from his house and told him Gatha was gone. When the prayer ended he suddenly began tapping his cane on the porch floor. He got to his feet, face flushed and tapped the cane faster and faster.

"That hound tried to bite her! I know he did. The boys were there, they seen it, they'll tell ya. Barking and growling all the time lately like he lost all sense. I should of beat hell out of him that day on the porch. That Blue Tick killed my Gatha! I just know he killed my sweet baby Gatha!"

Preacher Fuller looked at Pauley and Dylan. The boys rolled their eyes. Pauley tapped the side of his temple and said, "We never saw any such thing. He's touched." Grammy took George's hand, "George, you could probably use a good nap about now." She helped him inside to the back bedroom and left him to sleep. On the porch Preacher Fuller was telling Granddaddy that there was something not quite right about Gatha's passing. Pauley and Dylan listened intently.

"How could poor Miss Gatha be dead that long and George not know it?"

"Preacher Fuller, I hate to say this about my own kin— kin by marriage of course— and I hate to admit that I agree with these crazy wild-ass boys, but I believe George might a lost his mind. He'd have to of lost his mind to be living with a dead woman and giving her chocolates. When the funeral home came to get Gatha, Grammy and I went with them down to the house. There were candy wrappers all over the porch and a bag of chocolates in Gatha's lap. George must have been eating the candy himself. There's something else we aint told nobody. Grammy was trying to put the place in order and when she went to unplug and clean out that old deep freeze on the back porch she found George's hound. It was lying there on top of Gatha's bags of candy with its skull caved in. I tell you it's sad. Gatha may have passed peacefully in her rocker, but then you also got to think if George was out of his mind he could have done harm to her and his old hound. Yeah, this is a sad state of affairs and we may never know what happened."

Pauley had to grit his teeth to keep from smiling. It was going even better than he'd planned. They thought Aunt Gatha had died peacefully in her rocker or maybe Uncle George had simply lost his mind and did her and the hound in. Pauley felt home free, and while no one was looking he gave Dylan a thumbs up. Dylan didn't respond. He kept watching Preacher Fuller.

"It's still strange the way she went, sitting up in her rocker like that. Did Miss Gatha have a problem with her heart?"

"Heavens no," Grammy answered. "She was overweight, but I took her in for a checkup just a week before our trip. Doc Justin said for a woman her size she was as healthy as a horse. He said she'd probably out live us all, but the poor dear didn't. I guess the Lord had plans for her and decided to take her ahead of schedule."

Pauley was so close to laughing he dropped his head and covered his face with his hands. "Oh, Grammy," he thought, "It didn't have nothing to do with the Lord. Me and Dylan had plans for Aunt Gatha and the plan was a driving lesson in a '68 Chevy Impala that took her ahead of schedule." He wanted so badly to say this aloud but the plan was going so well—why lose it now?

"The Lord does work in mysterious ways, but I can't see the Lord taking a good Christian woman like Miss Gatha and letting her family find her that way. I believe there's something amiss in all this. I hope you folks won't be upset with me and I know it might not have been my place, but I talked with Mr. Gossett, the embalmer down at the funeral home. He said her body was in really bad shape due to decay, but he noticed what he suspected as bad swelling and bruising on Miss Gatha's forehead. You know in his line of work he'd be more likely to notice something like that quicker than we would." Preacher Fuller paused, then loosened the knot of his necktie. Grammy got up, went to him and took his hand.

"Preacher Fuller, you've been our pastor and Gatha's all these years. Nothing you could say would cause us to be upset with you. We know you loved my sister as much as we did and we appreciate you taking an interest in what happened to her. I think I can speak for all of us when I say we want to know any information you got from Mr. Gossett."

"I didn't want to bring this up before. I wanted all of you to have some time for grieving, but there just might be foul play involved. Maybe I should have said all this earlier, but I couldn't be for sure even after talking to Mr. Gossett. The Lord just now reached out and told me I had to give you this message. We've already laid her to rest but if I were you I'd think and pray on maybe exhuming the body and having an autopsy done to find out what really happened."

Pauley's heart sank right down to his knees. He wanted to scream, 'Shut up! Shut your damn mouth Preacher!' Granddaddy leaned forward in his chair, "Preacher Fuller, are you supposing that maybe George really did kill Gatha?"

"No, everyone knows he adored Miss Gatha. George may be a little off in the head but I don't believe for one minute he would have raised a hand to his wife. It could have been a drifter, someone with a cold heart passing through that did it. Hit poor Miss Gatha in the head and when the hound went to defend her he killed it the same way. Of course it could have been anybody with a cold heart that did it." The preacher looked across the porch at Pauley and Dylan. Pauley knew what he was thinking. The preacher was thinking it could have been those crazy wild-ass boys that did it.

"I can't make the decision for you and your family, but the Lord has told me today that as your minister I'm bound to advise you on this matter. If there's a possibility that Miss Gatha met with foul play you need to know and have the sheriff out here checking into it. You'll never know or have closure till they do an autopsy and find the cause of death. You owe it to Miss Gatha and the family, to try and find out."

Dylan looked at his brother. Pauley's fists were clenched; he was staring at the preacher. At that moment Dylan loved and hated his brother. "Me and you brother," he thought, "Both of us off-shoots of a bad match." It didn't matter. Nothing mattered now. Their mom and dad had deserted them. Any dreams they had were gone. Life was the farm, out here living in the sticks. Dylan knew that everything ended out in the cornfield the morning of the driving lesson. He thought of his dream in the cornfield and wished he had taken his mom's hand and danced with her, the delivery man, Aunt Gatha and the hound. Mom and the delivery man must be dead too and I could have joined them, out of this mess and…tapping, tapping, tapping. George was at the door, his cane thrust out, tapping and waving it at everyone on the porch.

"Ya find that murdering hound that done went and killed my sweet baby! Pauley, run down to the house and get my shotgun and load it. Dylan, ya get a flashlight and if it takes all night we'll find that sorry animal. I know his smell. I'll lead ya to him and ya boys can take my shotgun and blow his rotten head off. He killed my Gatha!"

George dropped his cane and broke into tears. Grammy went to him, "There's no need for that George, that old hound didn't kill Gatha. We were just going inside to pray and decide what to do next. If you like I can make you a snack and you can sit with us in the kitchen for prayer or maybe you'd like to nap a little longer."

"Don't make no difference to me, long as them boys find that damn hound and kill it."

Granddaddy got up to help Grammy get George back to the kitchen. "Preacher, give us a minute to get George settled. Grammy's gonna put out the leftover pie and a pitcher of cold milk, then we'll call you in for dessert and prayer."

Preacher Fuller took his handkerchief from his suit pocket and wiped his brow. "Yes boys, like your granddaddy said. This is a sad state of affairs. I'll never believe your Uncle George had anything to do with this. So almost a week passed without you boys so much as walking down the lane and checking on your aunt and uncle? I know you haven't been back to church till today mainly because of the embarrassment your mom Sue put on you, sitting in the back pew painting her nails and not listening to the gospel as a good Christian woman should do. But I want you boys to know that if there is anything you want to talk to me about I'm here for you, anything at all. The Holy Spirit is here for you too. No matter what you do or what you've done, if you confess it to the Holy Spirit he'll wash away your sins."

Pauley turned to Dylan and smiled, "You hear that Dylan? No matter what we do or have done, all we have to do is confess it to the Holy Spirit and he'll wash away our sins."

"Preacher Fuller."

"Yes son, I'm here for you."

"Do you drive?"

"No, Pauley, I don't. Small church and a small congregation within walking distance so I never saw the need to own a car or learn to drive."

Pauley stood and smiled down at Preacher Fuller. "I think the Lord just spoke to me like he spoke to you earlier. He sent me a message. He wants me to tell you that if you could drive you could reach sinners all across this county. Just think how pleased the Lord would be with you bringing all them sinners into his fold."

"Pauley, that's a good start. The Lord speaking to you and you thinking about the church and sinners. I hope to see you at this Sunday service." Preacher Fuller reached into his suit pocket and pulled out two small Bibles and held them out to Pauley and Dylan. "If you have time this week you might want to read some of Lord's teachings and after church service we could talk a little more about the Holy Spirit, and how he can lead you to salvation." Pauley and Dylan took the Bibles and stuffed them into the pockets of their jeans. Pauley lowered his head, staring at the floor of the porch.

"Preacher Fuller, you don't know how humbled I am right now that the Lord has used me as his messenger. You know we got a car down in the cornfield that needs a little work. Me and Dylan could fix it up and even teach you to drive. Get you started on the road to reaching out and bringing in all them sinners to your church."

"Pauley! Praise God! Now that's a real Christian way of thinking."

"Well, Preacher, the things you've said out here on the porch today really touched me. Got me to thinking about the future. I'm sure Granddaddy's gonna be busy with Uncle George for a while and I don't think he'd mind us borrowing his truck for your first driving lesson. What was that you said earlier about salvation, washing away sins no matter what you do? Maybe while I teach you to drive you could teach me how to confess my sins?"

Preacher Fuller took his handkerchief and dabbed at the sweat along his neckline. He turned to Dylan, confused. Dylan smiled, left the porch and started Granddaddy's truck.

VII.

The Light of Day

I'm glad you could come today. I know it's a long drive but I needed to talk with you. I had a perm put in yesterday. A new beauty shop opened up on Main. The young girl that works there did a good job on my hair. Oh, but listen to me go on—I didn't ask you to come to show off my new hairdo. I want to tell you about your daddy. You probably don't remember Walter. Of course you don't, you couldn't have been more than knee-high.

It's been thirty-five, maybe forty years ago, can't say for certain. I used to keep up with time, kept track of every passing minute. I used the beat of my heart as a guide. I'd count the beats and so many beats would equal a minute that had passed. Then I'd start on the next minute, my heart keeping time, counting off the seconds of one more minute.

You see, back then that's how I survived. I don't use my heart to keep time anymore. When you get old, time loses time and I am old. Yes, when you get old, time loses time and the next thing you know time and nothing else matters anymore. That's why I need to talk to you today about your daddy.

I met Walter my second year in high school. I knew I loved him the first time I saw him. He was the star of the high school football team. He stood six foot two, had sandy blonde hair, blue eyes and his body was one of disciplined muscle and grace. He could have had his pick of any girl, but he chose me. I was the envy of all the other girls that year.

I was pregnant before the year was out. Walter's mother Lila didn't like me but insisted we get married right away, saying "It had to be done to save face." Walter stayed in school but I dropped out because he wanted a stay-at- home wife and said I didn't need any more education for that. Sometimes I'd go to the games. Walter was headed to the football hall of fame. At least that's what everyone said, especially Lila. She would sit in the stands, decked out in lime green pants-suits and cheer Walter on to glory. I sat in the stands too, plump and round-bellied till my eighth month of pregnancy.

Lila barely tolerated me. She blamed me for every ball Walter fumbled, the long pass he missed and every kick that fell short of the goal post. I was the cause of all her son's shortcomings. To the day Lila died she continued to say that I was Walter's downfall in his run to the football hall of fame and glory. I never believed it.

I was a good wife.

I knew what tripped Walter on his run to the football hall of fame. It wasn't me, it was Walter himself. His senior year he got filled with his glory, filled with beer, filled with whiskey and fell on the field at the bottom of the heap rather than on the top. The coaches soured, the crowd soured and soon no one was cheering Walter on to glory. No one cheered except Lila. While the spectators yelled "Get the drunk off the field," she sat in the stands full of pride and cheered for her only child. She cheered right to the end when Walter finally staggered off the football field and climbed into the cab of an eighteen wheeler. He was washed up as a star player and had no choice but to get a trucking job to support his family. Lila said Walter was a star trucker. I never knew there was such a thing as a star trucker but that's what Lila told everyone he was.

Lila owned this rental house and the three acres it sits on. She kicked out the renters and deeded it all to Walter. The renters left most of their furniture behind and that old shed out back full of one thing or another. I found a little red wagon in the shed, its right front wheel was wobbly but I cleaned it up and used it to go for groceries while Walter was away. We didn't own a car, but I'd never learned to drive anyway. It was a two mile walk to town and I was grateful for the little wagon.

Lila changed gears. She went from cheering Walter on the football field to cheering him as a star trucker. She'd come over every night promptly at six and she and Walter would sit by the fire watching television and talk about how far he was destined to go in his new line of work. Walter would drink beer and Lila would sip thick, frosty Grasshoppers that were as lime green as her pants-suit. They watched the weather forecast at ten and if it was good Lila left happy. If the forecast was threatening she brooded about Walter being on the road the next day and how bad weather would put him behind schedule. Bad weather meant Lila stayed late into the night, drinking more Grasshoppers, brooding and checking maps for alternate routes for Walter's next run. You get the picture? For that reason I prayed daily for a good weather forecast.

Walter was on a ten day run when you were born. The day he came home I held you out to him. He walked right past me and you, went to his recliner by the fire and yelled, "Put it down and get me a beer." Walter had taken a partner that could help with the driving so he could do faster runs and take on more jobs. He'd met Roy at a bar in the next town over from us. At first the partnership seemed to be working. They got a lot of hauls and stayed on the road most of the time. But Roy liked drinking even more than Walter and they started getting in one kind of trouble or another while on the road. Reports started coming in and a lot of the companies they hauled for stopped contracting them.

When the hauls started drying up Walter and Roy spent their time out there in the living room drinking and watching football. After football season they took their drinking and guns out in the backyard. They built bonfires and set up cinder blocks lined with empty beer cans. Sometimes the guns fired all night long. Walter left all but one small patch of grass right off the back door of these three acres untended. Grass and weeds were waist high throughout the rest of the property and filled with snakes, rats and rabbits. If they had the misfortune to wander into the small yard they became new targets for Walter and Roy. They shot them and left them in the yard till morning and I buried them. There were more every day, the little yard littered with them.

Late that summer Walter and Roy built a small pen in the corner of the yard. The next day they came home with five wild-eyed Dobermans. When he was drinking—which was now all the time—he'd stand by the pen and toss in small bits of bone and scraps. It was barely enough for one dog, much less five. Walter would laugh as they fought, biting and tearing each other's flesh in competition for the pitiful bits of food. He hit them, too. He beat them daily with anything he could lay his hands on.

Walter was no longer a star trucker, at least not in my view. We never had enough money to live on. He was drinking more and missed a lot of the few hauls he got because he was too hungover or forgot what his schedule was. He resorted to borrowing money from Lila so we could put food on the table. Lila knew about the drinking, the missed hauls and the Dobermans but never said a word to Walter. Instead she accused me of wasting food, telling me she was paying for it and didn't want to find so much as a tablespoon of anything thrown out in the garbage. I no longer cared what Lila said.

I was a good wife.

Walter was always angry and now hitting me. It made no difference what I did or didn't do. If his beer was too warm or his dinner not warm enough he hit me. He hit me all the time. He didn't need a reason, he just liked hitting me. Why would a man enjoy hitting a woman? I don't know about other men, but with Walter I soon realized that under all that tall, blonde and muscle he was nothing more than a chicken. I still loved him.

You know, the funny thing is those dogs loved Walter, loved him just as I did. I'd watch from the kitchen window and when the sound of his diesel truck came up the driveway the

Dobermans would run to the corner of their pen and cringe. Then when Walter called out to them they'd go running to him, smiling dog smiles and wagging their wasted bodies. I'd cringe too. Walter would yell to me to bring him a beer and I'd go running, beer in hand, smiling and counting my heartbeats. We loved him. That's how time passed, me and those five starved dogs spending our days cringing and loving Walter.

Everyone knew what was going on. They saw the bruises and black eyes but never brought it up or asked me why or how. My grandmother came by often, bringing vegetables from her garden and giving me tips on how to stretch the small amount of food my budget allowed. She gave me some of her iron skillets, taught me how to season them and shared some of her recipes. She knew my situation and did everything she could to help me. One afternoon as we sat here in the kitchen having coffee she reached across the table, took my hand in hers and said, "Listen to me. You're going to be all right. You can make it as soon as you see the light of day." I didn't understand what she meant till that last night.

When winter came Walter and Roy got a three day haul and all I could think of was three beautiful days of peace. I made him a big breakfast of eggs the way he liked them, biscuits, grits, gravy and ham. He ate in silence, picked up his duffle bag, then halfway to the back door he turned.

"Clean this damn place up before I get home. There's a gallon bucket out next to the dog pen with their rations for the next three days. Don't give them one scrap more than what's in that bucket or so help me when I get home I'll beat you senseless."

The engine of the eighteen wheeler roared to life and at last he was gone, the house quiet. You were still asleep so I poured myself another cup of coffee and sat in the kitchen taking my time, sipping it slowly. The breakfast dishes could wait and Walter's orders to clean up the place could wait too. I needed this time alone and unafraid for just a little while. You woke up around six and after your breakfast I took the red wagon from the shed. I put a pillow in it, bundled you with blankets and laid you in it. Walter hadn't left me any money but I enjoyed going to town, looking in the shop windows and getting us both outside for fresh air.

On our way back home a neighbor had piled the edge of the street with all kinds of things for the trash truck to pick up. There was a small plastic kiddie pool on the top of the pile. By summer I thought it would be perfect for you. So I pulled you in the wagon with one hand and drug the kiddie pool with the other. When we got home I leaned it against the back of the house planning to wash it down and store it in the shed before Walter got home. I tried not to think of Walter, but I had learned how to be careful not to do or get anything that might make him mad. I made plans that night for me and you. Plans of everything fun we could do with the two days of peace left before he returned.

The sound of the Dobermans barking woke me at two the next morning. I hurried to the kitchen and turned on the porch light. Walter was getting out of Roy's car. He staggered to the back door, pushed his way past me and sat down heavily in one of the kitchen chairs. I stood silent. He was clearly angry.

"So what are you looking at? Are you wondering what I'm doing home two days early? Bring me a beer!" I got the beer and placed it on the table in front of him. He picked it up, blew on the top of it then shook it up and down. He pointed the beer in my direction and pulled the tab, spraying me with cold foam. He took one sip then threw the can across the room.

"Get me another, that one was flat." I took him the second beer. He pulled the tab and took a long drink, slamming the can down on the table and turning to me, his fist clenched.

"You been behaving? Cat got your tongue? Don't you want to know why I'm home?" He raised his fist so I nodded yes.

"Somebody stole the damn eighteen wheeler and the load! That's why I'm back here. Me and Roy stopped at a bar in Tennessee and that stupid asshole Roy left the keys in it. Can you believe the luck? I aint reported it to the contractor yet. I'm gonna meet up with Roy tomorrow morning at the diner and we're gonna go back to that bar and ask some questions. I'm taking my gun and if I find the bastard that took our truck I'm gonna kill him. You got nothing to say, huh? Smart girl. Get me another beer, go clean yourself up and make me something to eat."

I made him breakfast and he fell asleep on the couch. I kept you as quiet as possible and took you for a ride in the wagon, afraid to wake him. He was up by noon calling for another beer. Then he went out back, picked up a fallen limb that had snapped in half and beat the dogs. I put you down for a nap and went to the kitchen to watch him as he walked about the yard. He stopped and stood staring at the back of the house, then yelled for me to come outside.

He pointed at the kiddie pool and took another swallow of beer. "Where the hell did that come from? I didn't leave you no money."

"It was in the trash, Walter. I didn't buy it. I was going to clean it up and store it in the shed till summer for the baby. She'll be old enough for a little pool by then. It didn't cost us nothing." He backhanded me, sending me to the ground. He laughed.

"What do you think that slow-witted thing is gonna do in a pool? Probably tip over and drown. I've always had doubts it was mine. What'd you do, mess around on me or is it just slow like its mama? That pool's going in the dog pen. I'll fill it up once a week and save myself toting water. You better clean up and put something on the stove. Lila is on her way to hear the details about the truck."

I put together a skillet of beef and potato hash then laid the table with white bread, butter and a jar of my grandmother's canned sweet pickles. Walter and Lila barely touched the food—just went on out to the living room and sat by the fire talking and drinking their usual beers and Grasshoppers. They watched the early weather forecast at six. It was a good one so Lila left, assured that Walter and Roy would have good weather on their quest to find the truck.

I gave you dinner then pulled your high chair next to the sink so I could talk to you while I washed dishes. You were fussy that night. It could have been a touch of colic or maybe teething. Walter had changed the channel to wrestling and turned the volume up. You rubbed your cheeks with the back of your hand and whined. I took a washcloth, soaked it in cool water and gave it to you. You held it to your mouth and sucked the cool water. It seemed to ease you a little.

In the living room The Rock pinned someone to the mat and the crowd was going wild. Walter was yelling, "Yeah! Yeah, Rock you know how to do it!" I heard the sound of an empty beer can roll across the linoleum and dried my hands quickly. I opened another beer and placed it on the end table next to Walter's recliner. He didn't acknowledge me—just grabbed the beer and leaned forward as The Rock's manager entered the ring. I went back to the kitchen to finish the dishes and within minutes Walter was standing in the kitchen doorway, tapping on the woodwork. He yelled to be heard over the loud television.

"Match is over. The Rock won. I knew he would. That stupid Roy bet me a twenty that he'd lose this match. Roy is a real sawdust head. You aint finished yet? Hurry up and get that whining thing out of here. There's another match coming up and I don't want this playing in the background!"

I had just finished washing the big iron skillet that I'd used to serve up the hash to Walter and Lila. I couldn't remember the last time I had really looked at Walter, but for some reason that night I turned and looked at him standing in the doorway taking a sip of his beer, swaying and sneering. I didn't recognize him. Over the years the beer and whiskey had taken his body of disciplined muscle and grace, giving him in return pounds of extra flesh deposited in all the wrong places.

"Did you hear me? Get it out of here before the next match starts!"

I couldn't move, just stood there frozen, unable to take my eyes off him. You began to cry and his face went red. He threw his beer, hitting the cabinet between me and you and spraying us both with alcohol. Your cries turned to screams. He bolted across the room and struck you hard across the face. It was at that moment with the first small trickle of blood from your tiny nose—that I stopped counting—heartbeats and I knew what grandmother meant. I saw the light of day.

The light of day filled this kitchen; the room glowed as if lit up by stadium lights. Everything bright white, crystal clear, even the skillet in my hand. I swung and hit him in the left temple. In the light Walter looked as if he'd found glory again. His eyes went wide and he raised his hands to catch a long pass. I swung again and stopped him on the five yard line, the skillet making a sound like striking concrete. In my mind I've had a lot of "what ifs" about that night. I'd said my usual prayer for a good weather forecast so Lila would leave early. If the forecast had been bad Lila would have stayed, brooding and drinking Grasshoppers and maybe Walter wouldn't have hit you in front of his mother. Sometimes prayers are answered, but not always answered in the way you expect. I could have gone on taking Walter's hits but he shouldn't have hit you.

It took Lila three weeks of calling and asking about Walter and the truck before she reported him missing. The police questioned me and I told them the last time I saw Walter he was on his way to meet Roy at the diner and from there they were headed to Tennessee to look for the stolen truck. The police took Roy in for questioning. He told them Walter never showed up at the diner so he'd gone to look for the truck on his own. Roy was considered a suspect for months but the police never found any evidence to charge him with.

This house and land will be yours when I pass. You do what you want with it because time loses time and it doesn't matter anymore. I waited all these years to tell you, hoping you'd understand. I've tried to settle it all in my own mind for a long time but some things never settle. That's why I asked you to come today. I needed to tell you about Walter.

If you want you can go to the police when you leave here today, I would understand. After all is said and done he was your daddy. That's why I had my hair done yesterday just in case you decided to turn me in. You can tell the police the story but I doubt they'll believe you. Walter had a reputation for trouble. Everyone, including the police, assumed Walter had met a woman on the road and abandoned me and you. There was even a rumor that he'd got in a fight at a bar and someone had killed him. That's what they thought and few questions were asked. The whole thing died away quickly.

I was a good wife.

I've always cleaned my house with bleach. I like the scent of it. That night I scrubbed this house from top to bottom with four gallons of bleach. Bleach will wash away anything, even sins.

I was a good wife.

They never found his body. My grandmother taught me how to cut up a chicken nine different ways. I loved Walter. Those poor starved dogs loved Walter, too.

Jan Fink

VIII.

Hickory Nut America Park

"George McNutt's the name." McNutt set his beer on the bar and offered his hand to the young man sitting next to him. "Don't believe I've ever seen you round here."

"Bobby Owens, it's nice to meet you. I'm not from around here, in town for the day, covering the destruction of the park."

"Ah, a reporter," McNutt said with a grin. "And I suppose you'd be talking about Hickory Nut America Park?"

"Yes. My sympathy goes out to all you townspeople. A lot of planning and work must have gone into the designing and building of it; then to have it all destroyed in one day is tragic and sad."

"Tragic and sad?" McNutt threw back his head and bellowed with laughter. He beat his fist on the bar and slapped the reporter on the back, laughing harder, his eyes filling with tears.

"Son, it aint tragic and it sure aint sad. It's funny! Damn near the funniest event I ever witnessed." McNutt broke into uncontrollable laughter again.

Bobby looked at McNutt in complete bewilderment. McNutt tried to compose himself. He picked up his beer, took a long drink, then took his handkerchief from his shirt pocket and wiped the tears from his cheeks.

"Oh, I know what you're thinking. You're wondering how I could find such a thing so amusing. If you got a little time and can buy me another beer I'll tell you the whole story right from the beginning."

Bobby raised his hand and called out "Bartender" to the woman with multicolored hair sitting on a stool behind the bar. She walked toward them with a practiced sway of her hips. McNutt leaned in close to Bobby.

"She aint just the bartender, that's Jesse, the owner and manager of this establishment. I'd say she's pushing fifty but she's well preserved, don't you think?" Bobby nodded in agreement. "Look, Bobby boy, don't let her looks fool you.

Jesse is hard and tough as nails. She don't put up with no bullshit of any kind. I've seen her throw bigger men than me out of here for spitting on the floor. Yeah, Jesse is a real businesswoman. Likes things kept clean. She runs the best bar in town, course it's the only bar in Hickory Nut."

Jesse swayed up to McNutt and Bobby, propped one hand on her hip and reached out with the other taking Bobby's hand and shaking it hard enough to rattle his teeth.

"How you do? I'm Jesse. My bartender is out taking a pee but I guess I can get you boys a couple of cold ones. What'll it be?"

"Two of whatever Mr. McNutt's having." Jesse took the beers from the cooler and popped them open with one long red-polished nail.

"You boys enjoy." On her way back to her stool, Jesse glanced back at Bobby. "And by the way, young man, here's a tip for you. I wouldn't put too much store in what McNutt here tells you. The old coot aint been sober a day in his life." She winked and swayed her way over to her stool.

McNutt put his hand to his heart and gave a slight bow to Jesse's backside. "That woman truly does love me. You can hear it in all the sweet little things she says about me."

Bobby smiled, lifted his beer and took a short sip. The brand wasn't so bad. He'd been out in the sun all day and the cold beer rushed him. He felt relaxed for the first time that day. He'd reached Hickory Nut early morning and walked along the bank of what looked like a large lake, snapping photos of what was left of the park. His attempts to interview local residents who were at the park the day of the opening had offered up nothing but a lot of talk, but no one had given him a clue as to how the destruction of the park came down. He took another long drink from his beer feeling more relaxed. If there was a motel in town, he thought he'd have a few more beers and listen to the old coot McNutt. Couldn't hurt, maybe he did know how the park came to its end.

"You were saying, Mr. McNutt?"

"Just call me McNutt and I was saying. What was I saying? Oh yeah, I was saying how I could tell you the whole story about the park right from the beginning. Yep, Bobby, today is your lucky day. Just think, if you hadn't of come in here for a cold beer, you would a never had the chance to hear the true story. You come by accident, to the right place, at the right time and to the right source to tell you how Hickory Nut America Park came to be and how it ended. Funny how a thing like this happens, meeting up this way. When I said I'd tell you the story right from the beginning, I was speaking from experience. You see, I grew up with all the folks that hatched the idea, planned and built that park. I'll tell you about all of them because they were responsible for its birth and death."

McNutt pointed to his beer. "If you don't mind, Bobby?" Bobby ordered another round and a pack of cigarettes and opened his notebook.

"I knew from the start it would never work. It couldn't work because those folks have never gotten along. I'm assuming you're from the city so you may not understand some of what I'm going to tell you, but listen up. Small towns are different from cities. Small town folks are way too close to one another, everybody knows everybody's business. We were all born here in Hickory Nut and we've stayed here all our lives. New blood comes into town once in a while, but for the most part we end up marrying distant cousins. You might say we were all stewed in the same pot. That's one of the main reasons I never took a bride.

"Can I have one of your smokes? I aint a regular smoker, but I do like one with a cold beer and a good story. Now where was I? My theory, the only reason I can come up with to explain what has happened here in Hickory Nut in the past twenty-four hours. I enjoy watching people, always have. I was there that day, a long time ago in the beginning watching from across the street. Lula Dancing had just turned five and she was having a grand birthday party. I wasn't invited. It didn't make no difference to me because my mama and daddy couldn't afford a gift for Lula and I think she knew it and that was why I didn't get no invite. Lula was the great, great, great granddaughter of one of Hickory Nut's founding fathers. Every generation of the Dancings lived their entire lives in the old family home. The old house was bought up to date from one generation to the next, new plumbing, wiring and so on and extra bedrooms added when a generation had more young'uns than the house could hold.

"The Dancings were a proud bunch of folks, but paranoid as the day is long. Always afraid somebody was going to take away what they had. They had to maintain the best of everything. Be the best, that was their motto. Drove them all crazy. Drove the rest of us crazy too. Nobody ever got more or better than the Dancings. This was especially true with Lula. She was the pride of her daddy. In his eyes Lula could do no wrong. He used to take her to the carnival every year and push people aside with his cane saying, 'Step aside! Step aside! Lady coming through!' Naturally Lula loved the attention. She rubbed all our noses in the fact that she had more money and was better than us. Anyway, I wasn't invited to her party but I walked down to Main Street and watched the celebration from a distance.

"Destiny was not a word in my vocabulary or my understanding way back then, but I knew as I stood there watching the events of Lula's fifth birthday party that what was about to happen was just meant to be. Guess that's why I stood there on dry ground yesterday laughing when the whole park went down. It was a repeat of everything in the past right from the beginning. As I said, these folks never got along. I guess if you really had to name a catalyst or point a finger, you'd be pointing it right now at Lula Dancing. I was there and saw the first one to point a finger at Lula. No, now wait a minute, let me make this clear. It wasn't a finger. Missy Broughton pointed her tricycle at Lula."

# # #

The tricycle gained speed, racing down the grassy hill bordering the Broughton and Dancing yards. Missy's target was clear, crisp and white, glinting in the sun. Missy used the tricycle handle bars as sights, framing in Lula like a still photograph. Missy's feet, in large sleek black high heel pumps that belonged to her mother, pedaled faster and faster.

At the foot of the hill a group of children were attending Lula's grandiose celebration. Lula sat sideways on a gleaming new powder puff pink tricycle, her legs daintily crossed. She was dressed in crisp white linen with lacy socks to match and white patent leather shoes that seemed to need her constant attention. As she chatted with Percy she kept bending down, wiping them with her handkerchief, warding off even imaginary dust that might settle on them.

"Any more cake, Lula?"

"It's my birthday and I say no more cake. Besides, Daddy told me to watch you, Percy Smallwood. He said you'd eat the whole cake if I let you. So I say no more cake! My birthday and my birthday cake, so there, Percy, Percy!"

Percy hung his head and began to shuffle the old deposit slips he held in his hand. His father had given them to him to play with, and he had counted and cherished them and made them last. He pulled the stub of a number two pencil from his back pocket, thumbed through the stack of slips and found he only had three left that he hadn't written on. He sat on the ground next to Lula's shiny patent leather shoe and began to fill in the lines on the deposit slip. He wrote A's, B's, C's and 1, 2, 3's, then connected the letters at the bottom with loops that looked like small c's lying on their backs. He went back to the amount line and added as many zeroes as the line would hold next to 1,2,3. Then Percy signed his name, with each letter connected by the reclining c's. He was sad that he only had two slips left.

The party was getting boring and Lula said he couldn't have more cake. He thought about leaving the party early, his father might have more old deposit slips, but the sun had made him lazy. He decided to stay a little longer. Lula might change her mind and let him have more cake.

The other children drifted off to their own space, amusing themselves in the gardens and wading in the big concrete fountain Lula's daddy had had installed a week earlier. Joe Langston ripped away what was left of his shirttail. Earlier he had climbed one of the oaks in the garden and snagged his shirt on a ragged branch, ripping it straight across the back and most of the front. He'd found a sturdy forked stick and pushed it into the ground and leaned a few small twigs against it. He wrapped the remains of his shirttail around it making a splendid teepee. He was wondering if he could make Indians from stones and sticks when he first caught a glimpse of Missy in her wild ride down the hill. He watched her briefly, then went back to the problem at hand, how to make Indians.

Scooter Carlton and his dog Belch had taken refuge from the sun in the shade of one of the big oaks. Too much cake, ice cream and Lula had worn them both out. Belch was Scooter's best friend. You never saw one without the other. Belch was a Heinz fifty-seven, a dog of many. Scooter's daddy said he was mostly beagle and blue tick hound, but most would tell you he was just an ugly dog. When he barked a sound came out more like burping than barking, so Scooter's daddy named him Belch. He'd given Belch to Scooter because the dog wasn't good for nothing but keeping company. Belch stayed at Scooter's heels during the party and hadn't even offered to bite Lula when she kicked him, calling him a stinking old hound. Lula had insisted that Scooter take Belch home or tie him up, that he was ruining her party. Scooter refused to do either. Under the shade of the tree Belch lay with his head in Scooter's lap, licking the cake crumbs and ice cream stains on Scooter's trousers.

On the hill Missy's descent was going more rapidly than she expected. The tricycle had taken on a spirit of its own. Its wheels turned so rapidly that the pedals held Missy's oversized pumps, churning them round and round. Missy still had her target in sight. She talked to the tricycle, forcing her words into the wind.

"Yeah, you want to get Lula just as bad as I do. We'll show her who's got the fastest and best tricycle. Lula, always thinking she's got the best of everything. The best of everything? For once I'm gonna show Lula. I'm gonna show her. Gonna show you, Lula. I'm coming, Lula!"

Halfway down the hill the front wheel of the tricycle hit a large root. The wheel bounced upward, whirling in the air.

Missy's black pumps stayed with the pedals as the tricycle sped along on two back wheels till the front wheel came down with a thump. The landing sent Missy and the tricycle veering sharply to the right. She gripped the handle bars and brought down the heel of one sleek pump to regain balance. The heel hit the ground then ricocheted back into the air catching in the rear wheel spokes, hitting every spoke, making a sound like clackers. Belch raised his head and burped at Missy's clattering progress. Missy leaned to the left, gripping, clutching her toes and managed to hold the oversized pump on her foot. It sprang free from the spokes, dancing briefly in the air, then found its place back on the pedal. The shoe veered outward from the pedal like the angle of a badly planned roof, but held its mark. Missy regained her balance and pedaled on.

From the moment Missy pedaled her tricycle off the top of the hill, a sense of potentiality had filled her mind. She was younger than Lula but she knew she could lead her own parade. She became a show, a wonderful spectacle in her own mind. She was a warrior missile, her target locked in. Her ringlet curls flowed back from her face competing with the plastic streamers attached to the handle bars. Her Elvis charm bracelet jangled on her wrist, the charms bouncing, turning up the little framed portrait of Elvis, the hound dog, the guitar, then back to Elvis.

"This is going to be great, Elvis. Wish you were here!" Missy had even made up a little song for the occasion. She was near her destination. She pedaled faster and sang out.

Lula. Lula.

Went to the kitchen,

slipped on butter.

Hit her mother.

Now Lula aint Dancing no more.

# # #

"I tell you what, Bobby, it was something to see. I'll never forget Missy coming down off that hill, hair flying, eyes wide, that old tricycle of hers clattering away and her singing at the top of her lungs. For a moment I thought about yelling out, warning Lula, but didn't. Figured it served her right, being so high and mighty. I just stood there across the street watching destiny take its course."

McNutt pointed to the empty beer can in front of him. "Do you mind ordering up another round, son? All this talking has sort of dried me out." Bobby raised his hand to summon the bartender. A tall, surly young man with long black hair, an earring and snakeskin boots brought the beers.

"You running a tab?"

"Yes, I guess so. If that's okay?" The young man looked Bobby over, then turned to Jesse. "All right by you, Miss Jesse?"

"You run that young man a tab. McNutt here is telling him a story. You know McNutt's long-winded. They could be here all day. I wouldn't want him wearing out his pants pocket reaching in for six bucks every fifteen minutes. He can pay up at closing. I'm sure McNutt will keep him here till closing time with this tall tale he's spinning."

Bobby raised his beer to Jesse in a thank-you salute. He didn't know why he did. He felt strange about everything. Here he was at one o'clock in the afternoon sitting in a bar called The Nip, Sip and Gulp. He was close to being wasted on beer in the company of Dolly Parton and Waylon Jennings look-alikes on one side of the bar and McNutt on the other side telling him about some childhood memories.

"You all right, son?" McNutt took Bobby by the shoulder, turning him so he could see his face. "You need to take a break or maybe take a leak? You aint gonna throw up, are you?"

"No. I'm fine. I was just thinking."

"Good. I surely do hate when someone throws up during a story. I knew the first time I laid eyes on you that you were a young man who could hold his drink."

"Mr. McNutt, I don't see where all this is headed. I mean, well, what has a kid's birthday party got to do with the park?"

"Course you don't understand. City folks are always in a hurry. Cut to chase, get it done. Get to the point, you're thinking. That's why I told you earlier to listen up. I'm getting to the park, so listen. Now let's see, oh yeah, Missy coming down the hill like a guided missile. I've never seen a tricycle go that fast. Son, she was flat-out traveling. She hit Lula from behind. Lula never saw it coming. She was still sitting with her legs crossed arguing with Percy about cake when Missy's old red tricycle crashed into her brand-new powder puff pink trike. The crash sent her flying. She hit Percy first then bounced like a bright white ball of linen off of him, bouncing again and again, till the concrete wall of the fountain stopped her. The impact slowed Missy down a little, but didn't stop her. She bulldozed Lula's tricycle into the fountain wall a few feet from where Lula lay screaming. For a minute everybody froze. All you could hear was Lula screaming and Percy moaning.

"Joe was the first to make a move. Now, Joe Langston was one of those kind of kids that was always getting in trouble.

Poor kid often got blamed for things he didn't even do. You know the kind. Always in the wrong place at the right time.

"Well, Joe must have thought he was going to catch the blame so he got up and ran. When he reached the table with the cake, ice cream and punch, he bumped into it. What was left of his shirt caught on the edge of the table, pulling it over, dumping cake, ice cream and red punch all over Percy. The table trailed along behind Joe for a few feet till his shirt gave up and ripped clean off his back. Joe never looked back. He kept on running half naked out of the yard and down the street.

"Belch decided that since the birthday refreshments were on the ground, or more to the point, they were on Percy who was on the ground, he was free to help himself. He ran from under the oak and set in. Percy had all the wind knocked out of him when Lula bounced on him, but Belch brought him around licking his face. When Percy looked down and saw that red punch all over him he thought he'd been killed and started screaming along with Lula, 'Help me! I've been killed and Scooter's dog is eating me up!' At that point I damn near came close to wetting my pants.

"Now Missy must have known her moment of triumph was over. She up and ran just like Joe. The rest of the kids at the party knew something bad was about to come down and followed behind her. When Lula's daddy reached the yard, the only ones left were Lula and Percy lying there screaming, Belch eating cake and Scooter standing under the oak, hands in his pockets. Lula's mama cleaned Percy up and sent him home. Lula's daddy rushed her over to Doc Pricket's office. She was bruised up and had to have a couple of stitches in her forehead but was otherwise okay.

"Another round here, Bobby buddy?"

"Sure. Bartender, keep them coming!"

McNutt leaned close to Bobby and whispered, "I don't like that long-haired kid. He gotta attitude, you know what I mean? Wish Jesse had never hired him. I hope he don't last long cause I like a smile with my beer order."

"Yes. I think I do know what you mean. He wouldn't win a popularity contest, that's for sure." McNutt slapped him on his back, laughing loudly. "So I'm guessing Missy was in big trouble?"

"Oh yeah. You got that right. Things were never the same after that day. It started out slow like most things in a small town but it grew and has lasted to this day. Missy was pretty much banished. She couldn't even set one foot on the Dancings' property. Lula's daddy said Missy had scarred his baby girl for life and was a danger to society. He took Lula out of public school and brought in tutors so she'd never have to encounter the likes of Missy again. Old man Dancing made it hard for Missy's folks too. Went around telling everyone in town they ought not to let their children play with that Broughton girl. He told them Missy was dangerous and crazy and might turn on their children at any moment. Lots of people listened and stopped letting Missy play with their kids. Blackballed that little girl. That's what they did to Missy. It was bad between the Dancings and the Broughtons from that day on. It didn't get any better over the years. The two warring families brought in the rest of the community, folks choosing sides, adding to their numbers, and that's the way it went when we were all growing up and it continues to this day.

"All of us grew up and went our own way, but not too far away. None of us ever left Hickory Nut. Not for good anyways. Oh, we went here and there but always came back to Hickory Nut. Percy never married. He figured living was cheaper without a wife. Between me, you, Bobby, and the fence post there's been talk of him and Miss Jesse keeping time together, but that don't mean marrying if you know what I mean. Percy's now the mayor of Hickory Nut. He was always good with numbers, money and such, he does a good job.

"Now Lula, her daddy thought he'd picked the perfect husband for his little princess. Lester that was his name. Lester's family had more money than the Dancings had pride.

You got to know that perked up old man Dancing's ears to a sharp point. Lester's daddy had sent him fresh out of high school in Atlanta, Georgia, to Hickory Nut to open up a lumber yard. Lester's daddy was the king of southeastern lumber and he'd made a fortune from it. Guess he figured Lester would follow in his footsteps, but what he didn't figure on was Lester getting caught up in the clutches of the Dancings. From the beginning poor Lester had three strikes against him that made him open season for old man Dancing. Lester was rich, young and available. The Dancings snatched him up and married him off to Lula before he cut his first piece of lumber.

"Now son, you being an educated man, I'd guess you'd have to be right smart doing reporting work. You may not give me credit for having a lot of sense. You're probably saying to yourself, Old McNutt, he's got only one oar in the water, but I tell you what, I had enough sense to know that a marriage made of money and pride don't make for happiness. Lester and Lula stayed married long enough to have two children, a boy and a girl. One night about eight o'clock he told Lula he was going back to the lumber yard to check on a few things and nobody in Hickory Nut has seen him since.

"Hey, you still with me, Bobby? Looks like you're having a sinking spell."

Bobby attempted to focus his eyes. He thought of ordering coffee, but doubted caffeine would help. He took another sip of beer and looked at McNutt, squinting till he saw only one McNutt. As long as he squinted he could focus on the center McNutt while the other two blurred in and out to the right and left, like 3-D ghosts. He hadn't realized till that moment how very much McNutt looked like Clark Gable. The center McNutt stared back at him with jet black hair, chiseled face and thin mustache. The resemblance was damn near scary.

"Mc, McNutt. Say, frankly, my dear, I don't give a damn." Bobby squinted harder and leaned into what he hoped was the center McNutt's face and waited.

"What?"

"Mr. McNutt, did anyone ever tell you that you bear a striking resemblance to the late great Clark Gable?"

"No, Bobby, not in this lifetime."

"Well, you do. And you know something else. I'm glad I met you, old buddy. Glad I met you." Bobby twirled around on his barstool. He circled around twice, catching glimpses of McNutt, the 3-D ghosts, Jesse and the bartender. Then he stopped the spinning stool by grabbing the bar with one hand. He ended up facing the tables surrounding the dance floor. Two locals in dirty overalls sat at the third table nearest the bar.

They watched Bobby with beers half raised to their lips. Once he got his balance Bobby held up his beer and pulled his cigarette lighter from his shirt pocket. He raised the Bic even with the beer and flicked it on. He got to his feet waving the Bic and beer above his head, his feet moving in a voodoo rendition of the Statue of Liberty dancing.

"Okay, lis, listen up. I, I, Bobby Owens, am sitting next to the one and only, that hunk of the silver screen, that heartthrob of all time. Yes, ladies and gents, you guessed it. I am sitting next to the reincarnate of the beloved CLARK GABLE!"

Jesse was on her feet and McNutt could tell she meant business.

"McNutt, you've gone and got this young man drunk as a dumpster. You settle him down or the two of you will have to leave!" Jesse waved to the two men in overalls. "Edgar, Luke, ya'll don't pay no nevermind to McNutt's friend here. He's just a little tipsy, wouldn't hurt nobody or nothing. He's having a little too much fun, that's all. I'm gonna send over a couple of beers to you, on the house." Jesse held up two fingers to the bartender and pointed to Edgar and Luke's table. Then she turned back to McNutt.

"You gonna settle him down?"

"Sure, Jesse. I think he could use some fresh air. I'll take him for a tour of Hickory Nut. Can we get a large coffee and a couple of sixpacks to go? Come on, Bobby. I'm gonna show you the town."

"Show me what, Clark? What show we gonna see?"

McNutt took Bobby by the arm and hoisted him from his barstool. Bobby was unsteady on his feet, but McNutt was strong. He'd spent time in the lumber yard, the same lumber yard owned by Lula's husband, Lester. Back then McNutt had stood in line beside men younger than him all eager for work and was surprised when his number was called. For the next three years he got up at three in the morning and spent his days lifting, sweating and running pine and oak through the blade of the saw. At the end of the day he went home exhausted, smelling of pine resin and sawdust, but it was work and a paycheck every two weeks. That was a part of the story he hadn't shared with Bobby. But for now all he wanted was to sober Bobby up enough to get the story of Hickory Nut America Park told.

Jesse was waiting at the door holding the coffee and the sixpacks in a brown paper bag. "Your friend gonna pay the tab now?"

"Keep it running. I'll be back, sweet Jesse." McNutt blew her a kiss. Jesse shoved the paper bag into his chest and turned back to the bar. McNutt watched her hips sway away and under his breath said, "My, how I do love that woman."

McNutt half carried, half dragged Bobby across the parking lot. He had no idea what Bobby had arrived in but suspected it was the white Volvo parked alongside Edgar and Luke's beat-up Ford pickup. He decided to take his own car, a vintage 1961 Lincoln Continental with suicide doors. It was his pride and joy and the only outlaw status he had ever successfully gained and maintained. He'd bought it off old man Dancing ten years after the model had been proclaimed a hazard to its occupants. To McNutt's knowledge it had never truly posed a threat to the Dancing family. The fact was that one day while on an outing Lula told her daddy that she thought the back door was trying to open on its own and throw her to the street.

After that day the white Lincoln had sat in the Dancings' backyard with the tires dry rotting till McNutt offered old man Dancing one hundred fifty dollars to haul it away. He took it home and restored it. It was the one true, lasting love of his life and he wanted to provide for it in the future when he died. He checked into burial plots at Hickory Nut's oldest cemetery. The plots were four by eight feet. By his calculations he would need five plots. That would be enough room for burying the Lincoln with him in the driver's seat. He'd bought the plots on credit and was still making monthly payments.

McNutt put Bobby in the passenger seat, handed him the coffee and placed the brown bag of beer between them. He started the Lincoln, and Bobby fell to his left leaning on the beer, reaching out for McNutt's arm.

"You, you know what? I think I'll ca, call you Mr. Clark Mc, McGable Nutt. Whada you think?"

"You call me anything you want, long as you call me. Our first stop of the tour will be Lula Dancing. You might want to fasten your seat belt, buddy."

McNutt drove to the town square and parked in front of a sprawling plantation surrounded by boxwoods and white picket fencing.

"Here we are, Bobby. This is where it all started. See that hill? That's the one Missy road her tricycle down and started the war. Her house used to be right on the other side of that hill but it's gone now. Burned to the ground about ten years ago. Missy still owns the land but she's living on the outskirts of town now."

"Whoa! You said the Dancings had money but this looks like the White House! Who lives in a house like this?"

"You're sounding better, coffee's doing its job. Lula still lives in that house. Now I think the last thing I told you about the Dancings was when Lester disappeared. Lula had her daddy drag the lake, search the woods, you name it, it was done. None of the efforts turned up Lester, dead or alive. Some of the town folk say he went back to Atlanta, used his daddy's money and influence and got a divorce from Lula and remarried. You'd never get one of the Dancings to confess to such. They closed down the lumber yard.

"Lula did her best to raise the boy and girl, but was hardly good at it. She was a grown woman but still operating with a selfish child mind. Michael, the son, was killed in a car wreck, his blood alcohol numbers off the chart. The girl, Polly, she lay down with every man that crossed her path, so old man Dancing had Lula put her out on the street. No grandchild of his was going to cause disgrace to the Dancing name. Polly stayed here and there long enough to get pregnant and disappeared just like Lester. Lula's mama and daddy passed years back, so now Lula lives in that big rambling house by herself with a bevy of maids and groundskeepers."

McNutt drove east, then five miles out of town he parked in front of Missy's house. He opened two beers and handed one to Bobby.

"All right, here we are at the second stop of our tour. This is where Missy lives now. That's a nice, practical little ranch style house, don't you think? In spite of all that old man Dancing tried to do to put the black ball on her and make it stick, she did pretty well. Married Billy Long and had five kids, all of them healthy good stock. Billy owns and runs the City Café. You probably passed it on the way to the bar. Best food you can get in Hickory Nut. Missy helps him during dinner rush. She runs the cash register for Billy in the evenings and works days as the town clerk. She and Percy pretty much run this town between the two of them. I'm right proud of her, but you can imagine how Lula feels about Missy ending up with more power than she has. Percy's house is a mile or so down the road. I'll drive you by. I see him once in a while at the bar and have a few beers with him, but other than that he stays pretty much to himself. Busy with mayor stuff.

"We're gonna head back to town now and hit the back streets and alleys. If we're lucky we might find Joe. He don't have a home, stays here and there. Spends most of his time with Julia Finley. Julia is Hickory Nuts' bag lady. She's got a tent out behind a rundown abandoned storage building downtown. It's not much more than a barn, left untouched for years, to some an eyesore and others a mystery. There are places where the boards have separated from its weight, leaving peepholes. Aint nothing in it now but a swarm of feral cats, birds and bats roosting in the eaves. Julia spends most of her time panhandling with Joe and going through people's trash barrels salvaging things and reselling them."

McNutt drove through every back street and alley, even checked out the tent behind the storage building. Bobby was feeling better, getting his second buzz on his second beer.

"I don't know where he could be. Guess I'll take you on to our next destination. That'd be Scooter Carlton's place, close to the lake and where the park was built. It's out of town so we got a little ways to go, might as well tell you about Joe on the way.

"Besides me, Joe Langston and Scooter Carlton were the only two who were spared being pulled into the war between the Dancings and the Broughtons. We didn't feel no need to join up with either side.

"Joe quit school, left Hickory Nut in the early sixties. He went north, looking for work, didn't find work but became a part of the Love Generation. He went to Woodstock, marched on Washington, met Thai stick, LSD and hashish, and soon forgot what he went north for. He eventually came back to Hickory Nut, an aged, worn-out hippie. He ran a record shop here for a while till the police investigated him. The locals started complaining, they thought he might be selling records out the front door and drugs out the back. It wasn't true but the police shut him down anyway. After that he roamed the streets. Life sorta beat Joe. When he couldn't get drugs he got to drinking heavy. Nowadays he spends all his time with Thunderbird and Night Train Express.

"Hey! Wait a minute, Bobby, we're in luck. That's him over there in the Piggly Wiggly parking lot panhandling with Julia. We'll make a quick stop, I want you to meet him and see what a small town can do to people."

McNutt turned into the parking lot and pulled up alongside Joe and Julia. Joe was thin, dirty, wearing faded ripped jeans and a Magical Mystery Tour T-shirt that was riddled with holes. Julia, short and round with thinning faded red hair, was dressed in polyester pants cut off the knees, a Nike T-shirt, worn-out Reeboks, her neck, arms and ankles draped in costume jewelry. They approached the Lincoln, hands out.

"Hey man, can you spare us a little change?"

"Joe. It's me, George McNutt." Joe hesitated, looking in through the car window. Julia went on to the car behind them, her hand out, asking for change.

"Oh yeah, man! I remember you. Dude, you got a nice ride here."

"I want you to meet a friend of mine. This is Bobby. He's a reporter in town for the day doing a story." Joe backed away from the car holding his hands above his head.

"Look, man! I aint done nothing! I'm clean!"

"Joe, he's doing a story about the park."

"Wow! We gotta park? How cool is that?"

McNutt reached in his pocket, pulled out a twenty and held it out the car window. "Here, Joe. You and Julia take this, get you some food and go on back to your tent before the law comes and runs you off."

Joe grabbed the twenty, backed away bowing and giving the peace sign.

"All right, man! Peace! Peace like a river! I marched on Washington, dude. Did you know that, dude?"

"Yeah, Joe, I remember hearing you marched on Washington." Joe smiled bad teeth and ran to Julia waving the twenty.

"McNutt, that was pretty damn sad."

"I know. That's what I wanted you to see, that's what a small town does to some. And Bobby, I bet you every dime I got in my pocket that twenty will go for Thunderbird and Night Train

Express. Joe and old Julia will be drunk as chickens before we reach Scooter's house. Mister, I know a deadbeat when I see one and that's what poor Joe became.

"I think you'll like Scooter. Hell, he's a story in his own right. Out of all of us including Joe, I'd have to say Scooter had it the roughest. He left Hickory Nut after graduation. Attended college, got a degree in English literature and came back home to teach at the local high school. That was a mistake, he should have never come back here. He was a good teacher, a little slow in getting his points across but a good teacher. It was in his third year teaching that one day some of his students locked him in the supply closet at the close of the school one Friday. It was just a high school prank, maybe they thought Scooter had a key and could get out, but he didn't have a key. He stayed locked in that closet all weekend. Come Monday when one of the staff found him he'd had a mild stroke. It left him with a permanent stutter, a slight limp and a love of explosives. He never went back to teaching. Things started blowing up around the school. Four dumpsters, part of the football field and then the flag pole. Folks knew it was Scooter but they felt bad about what the kids had done to him, hoping he'd get it out of his system and go on with life. That wasn't true when it came to Lula. She convinced herself that he was going to blow up her house so she had the police talk to him and give him a choice.

He could stop blowing things up or go to jail. Scooter had had it with the whole town and packed up and moved out next to the lake. He's living with pack of dogs in an isolated, rundown old shack."

McNutt drove uphill till the road turned into little more than a cattle path, then stopped the car. "We'll have to hoof it from here, Bobby. I aint about to scratch up my baby trying to drive any further." They reached the hilltop and what was left of a log cabin, its walls and roof patched with everything from cardboard and wood pallets to car parts. The yard was littered with arcade games and folding chairs, polyester tent canopies hung from the trees like over-sized ghostly apparitions. A half dozen scraggly dogs ran toward them announcing their arrival. McNutt put his hand out, stopping Bobby. "Hold up a minute till I call out. He's got part of this place booby-trapped!"

"Scooter! Scooter Carlton! It's me, McNutt, and a friend! All clear, Scooter?" The cabin door opened and a small man with graying temples leaned out.

"C-c-c-clear o-o-on t-t-the p-p-p-path! D-d-d-dog's d-d-don't b- b-b-bite!"

"Scooter, this here is Bobby Owens. He's in town doing a story about the park. I've been taking him for a tour of Hickory Nut. Took him by Lula, Missy and Percy's house and we ran into that pitiful Joe down at the Piggly Wiggly. I wanted him to meet you too." Scooter gave Bobby a concerned look then reached out to shake his hand.

"Y-y-y-you m-m-meet L-l-l-lula?"

"No, McNutt showed me where she lived."

"G-g-g-good. Y-y-y-you l-l-l-look h-h-h-her i-i-in t-t-the e-e-eye a-a-and s-s-s-she t-t-t-turns y-y-y-you t-t-to s-s-s-stone!" McNutt laughed and slapped Scooter on the back.

"You got that right, Scooter. What are doing with all this stuff in your yard?"

"W-w-w-washed u-u-up f-f-f-from t-t-the p-p-p-park. G-g-g-gonna u-u-use t-t-to p-p-p-patch t-t-the r-r-r-roof. Y-y-y-you w-w-w-want t-t-to c-c-c-come i-i-in? I-i-i-i c-c-can b-b-b-build u-u-us a-a-a f-f-f-fire. I-i-i-i g-g-got s-s-s-some w-w-w-weenies."

"No thanks. We've got one more stop before I take Bobby back to his car. Just wanted to stop in and let him meet you. You be good, Scooter, see you later, buddy."

"Y-y-y-you t-t-t-too."

McNutt drove Bobby south along back roads till they reached the park site. He parked and pulled out the second sixpack, popping two open and handing one to Bobby.

"Well, this is it. The end of my story about Hickory Nut America Park. This seventy-five acres has always been flood prone. Even during droughts there's standing water, but this is where Percy and Missy chose to build the park. They called a big town meeting and proposed the idea. Percy and Missy thought the park would bring folks to Hickory Nut and when they came they'd bring their wallets. The two had already come up with the name for the park and of course Lula objected. She felt it should be named after her great, great, great grandfather, Ezra Harrison Dancing, who founded Hickory Nut. They put the motion on the table but it was voted down. People were tired of Lula and made it clear with their votes that the park would not bear the Dancing name.

"You think that stopped Lula? She was determined to get the Dancing name affiliated with the park in one way or another. And she knew just how to draw Percy in. Money! Lula told him she'd pay for all the landscaping if they placed a plaque at the entrance of the park saying it was all donated by the Dancing family in honor of Ezra Harrison Dancing, Founding Father. Percy could hardly say no, the town didn't have a lot of money in its treasury in spite of Percy's notorious penny pinching. So as you see, as usual, Lula got her way. Bobby, you see that little replica of the Eiffel Tower out in the middle of the water?"

"Is that what that is? I took a photo of it this morning. I liked the American flag flying at the top, 'all that was left' kind of shot. Good composition."

"It's pretty much all but covered with water, but that's what it is. That was Lula's idea. Now what the Eiffel Tower's got to do with Hickory Nut America Park I don't have a clue. But she was putting out the money and the town let her do as she liked. I thought the tower was ridiculous but I gotta say the rest of the landscaping was pretty impressive. Lula put boxwoods, dogwood trees and all kinds of blooming plants throughout the park. I got ahead of myself here, I aint told you how they solved the standing water problem. They built a little dam up there real close to Scooter's cabin up on the hill. Most of the town folk would tell you that the flood was Percy's fault because he built the dam on the cheap. Like most things in Hickory Nut the concrete had been poured into a maze of uncertain materials. But I'm here to tell you the flood was not Percy's fault.

"The rain came just as the last of the concrete set up. In Hickory Nut the rain comes once a year, and lots of it. That the rain had come at this time was a blessing to some and a curse to others. The park had been completed, the sodded grass was green and the plants were in full bloom. The Eiffel Tower looked down on a rose garden in the shape of an American flag, the blue in the flag made of dark, almost black hybrid roses. There were walking trails, picnic tables, concession stands and a playground for little kids with a merry-go-round, a slide and everything from skunks to raccoons on giant springs that tilted and swayed. To the right over there was an open arcade lit by Japanese lanterns with games and a fifties jukebox tucked in one corner. It was a beaut of a park, but like I said it was doomed from the beginning. Hand me another beer, Bobby.

"When I said the rain was a curse to others, I was talking about Scooter and his pack of dogs. It was a slow rain at first and the water started to rise back there at the foot of the hill where Scooter lives. When the rain got heavy the dam held, the park stayed dry but the water kept rising till it was almost at Scooter's front door. Of course it was a threat to Scooter and Scooter handled it just like he did the high school. The day of the grand opening he loaded up his little fishing boat with dynamite and rowed out to the center of the dam and waited."

"You're kidding? Come on, McNutt, you are kidding, right?"

"Well, Bobby, I promised you the real story of Hickory Nut America Park and I aint kidding. I'm telling it just the way it came down. I'm gonna go ahead and ask you not to quote me when it comes to Scooter's part of the story. You met him, this town took him down just like it did Joe."

"But how can I tell the real story and leave Scooter out?"

"I heard one time that writers can take what they call artistic license sometimes and can swing a story in a different way. I guess that's what I'm asking you to do because Scooter don't need no trouble. When he moved out of town all he wanted was to live his life out up there on the hill with his dogs. Percy, Missy and Lula knew the water would rise and take his home and they didn't care as long as their precious park stayed dry. So can I have your word, Bobby, that you'll swing the story?"

"This is totally unethical, but yeah, McNutt, you've got my word. I'll swing it."

"Good deal. Bobby, you see that big pine behind us to your right?"

"Yeah."

"That was where I was standing and watching the grand opening. The rain had slowed to a mist but it was still coming down. The whole town came to see Percy with Lula and Missy standing at his side, cut the ribbon while the high school band played 'God Bless America'. When the song ended the blast came. To this day I don't know how Scooter managed to set off the dynamite without blowing himself up, but he did. With the noise of the explosion still ringing in our ears, time froze for a few minutes, then came the sound of rushing water. People were running in all directions. When the water got waist high Percy abandoned Lula and Missy and climbed up the little Eiffel Tower out there. Fire department had to take a boat out and rescue him that afternoon.

"Lula managed to hang on to one of the support posts of the open arcade till Missy floated up next to her. Missy tried to grab the post but missed, and her hand ended up lodged in Lula's hair. Her hand caught in Lula's shield of Aqua Net Hair Spray and she held on till Lula's hair snapped and sent both of them downstream. When Lula waded out of the water she looked like an unkempt sheepdog."

"Was anyone hurt?"

"Nay, only thing hurt that day was pride. You see why I said the destruction of the park was damn near the funniest event I ever witnessed. Right up there with the day I watched Missy take her famous ride off the hill into Lula and her new tricycle.

"So that's the story, Bobby. Percy and Missy got their pride hurt and a big dent was put in the city coffer. What the town folk didn't know was the park was never insured. Lula of course never recovered any of the money spent for landscaping and was embarrassed by the whole event. Lula had plenty of money to lose and embarrassment wasn't something that stuck with her for long, she was a Dancing. With that said, I guess I better be getting you back to town."

McNutt pulled alongside Bobby's Volvo and turned off the ignition. "How'd you know this was my car?"

"I told you. I watch people. Always have and you can figure things out about a person by watching them."

Bobby reached over and shook McNutt's hand. "I thank you for the tour and the story. I've got to head back to the city. Here's a hundred, that should cover my tab. I've got to say you are a real piece of work, McNutt."

"Well, I thank you for that. And I thank you for swinging the story. Means a lot to me. Scooter's a real good friend." McNutt tore off a piece of the paper bag that held the empty beer cans, reached in his pocket, pulled out a pen and wrote his name and address on it.

"I don't take the paper but sure would appreciate you sending me a copy of your article. You might want to hang on to my name and address. There aint much news here in Hickory Nut but I have a feeling you may have one more story to cover in this little town someday." McNutt leaned against the Lincoln waving till Bobby was out of sight.

"I told you I'd be back, Miss Jesse."

"Where's that friend of yours? He's got a tab, you know!" McNutt handed her the hundred and ordered a beer.

"What kind of lies did you fill that poor young man's head with?"

"I told him nothing but the truth, Jesse."

"The truth according to George McNutt, I suppose. Oh, I almost forgot. That young man left his notebook here. Maybe you can run out and catch him before he leaves."

"I'll hold on to it, Miss Jesse. Bobby's gonna be back to do another story one of these days. He's gonna write my story and my obituary."

"What in heaven's name are you talking about, McNutt?"

"Bobby's gonna come back when I'm buried in my Lincoln out in the Hickory Nut Cemetery. Now don't you know that's gonna be one fine story?"

IX.

The Freer

The first time I saw Buzz I was working an accident out on a stretch of highway that the locals called Death Road. The police scanner next to our bed had gone off at eleven that night. I heard the location and knew Death Road had claimed another victim. It took all my energy to climb out of bed, grab my camera and notebook and drive the three miles to the scene.

Blue lights flashed to the right and left, blocking traffic north and south. I showed my reporter's badge and the police chief grudgingly waved me through the barricades. A young Hispanic man was lying crumpled across the white line. His car had taken flight to the opposite side of the road, landing upside down in the ditch amid road litter of beer cans and fast food wrappers. The road had hills, blind spots where little roads sprouted along each side, most of them dirt road tributaries unmarked by stop signs or street lights to warn a weary traveler of the main stream of traffic ahead on Death Road.

Yards down from where the young man's car lay, an old black man was leaning against a beat-up brown 1970s Oldsmobile Delta 88, a tank of a car, built to last. The entire backseat and window ledge were filled with Happy Meal toys. I approached him, hoping for an interview. He didn't seem to be aware of me. He was wearing four shirts, each of the sleeves folded up separately above his elbows. Along both forearms were wrist watches, I counted twenty-four in all.

"Excuse me. Were you involved in the accident?" He still didn't acknowledge me, his attention focused on the watch near his left elbow.

"Excuse me. Were you in the accident?"

"Nossir."

"Did you see the accident happen?"

"Nossir

I suspected he was a nut job or an ambulance chaser. I wrote up the accident location, took a photo of police lights flashing and went home.

My wife, Sarah, and I had been in Blount County, Alabama, a year. We'd met in Manhattan three years earlier. She was the first Southern girl I'd ever known and I fell hard for her charm and wit. We were married within a month. She was attending school at The Fashion Institute of Technology and I was working for a newspaper. When Sarah became pregnant with our twins she was ready to go back home to her family and the South. She had seen little kids on the streets of Manhattan trussed up in harnesses and being led around like pets and wanted nothing to do with it. Sarah quit school, I gave my notice at the newspaper, and we packed up and moved to this rural Alabama county at the foothills of the Appalachian Mountains.

Twin girls, Christie and Carrie, were born three months after we arrived. Sarah was happy being near her family but I can't say the same for me. I had an impressive resume and was able to get on with the county paper, but found myself in the land of the South, a place so foreign, I had difficulty getting the gist of language and manner. The most devastating was the lack of any investigative reporting or any other leads that had any meat to them at all. Being the "new boy" and a Yankee to boot, I was sent out on accident calls when I wasn't in the office proofreading and writing obituaries.

Night after night the police scanner sang, calling me to stretches along Death Road, crushed cars and trucks and more crumpled bodies. True to its nickname, Death Road kept taking lives. The odd thing was the old man was there at every accident. Like the first time I saw him, leaning against the beat-up Oldsmobile, checking the watches along his arms. I decided to approach him again. I put out my hand; he hesitated, then gripped mine, shaking it roughly up and down.

"My name's James. I'm a reporter."

"Yessir, I knowed you was. James that a good Christian name. A book in the Bible."

"I don't know much about the Bible, don't attend church, not a religious man. I drink, smoke and cuss. Guess my mother had a sense of humor when she named me. And your name?"

"Buzz."

"Well, Buzz, every time I come out to one of these accidents you're always here. Are you a curiosity seeker?"

"Not real sure what that is but I gotta say no."

"Then why are you out here on Death Road every night?"

He looked down at one of his watches then up at me and smiled. "It was nice talkin with you, James, but I gotta go now and do some cookin. I be seein you soon."

He started the Olds, turned and waved, then headed north and out of sight. I was a bit annoyed that I had wasted my time but also intrigued by the old man. As busy as Sarah was with the twins she sensed my frustration with the new job. I had told her about the old man and one night after she got the girls to sleep she suggested that I talk to him again, that there might be a good human interest story in him. I saw him four more times along Death Road before I asked him if he'd like to meet me downtown the next day for a cup of coffee or maybe lunch. He agreed to meet me down the street from the diner. I got there half an hour early, waiting and anxious that he might not show, but he was there, right down to the minute we'd planned, parking the Olds a few spaces behind my car. He joined me on the sidewalk, smiling and looking up at the sky.

"It a good day for a meetin."

"That it is. Have you ever eaten at the diner? The food's not too bad."

"That diner been here a long time but I aint never eat there. You knows I guess that black peoples not allowed back in them years to eat with white peoples. I knows they can now but I aint ever had no company to eat with till today."

We walked along looking in shop windows filled with plastic Easter eggs, bunnies and artificial green grass dripping from pastel baskets filled with tooth decay assortments of sugar and chocolate coated candies. I told Buzz I had twin girls and looking at the displays made me grateful they hadn't discovered their sweet tooth yet.

"My daddy used to give me a piece a sugar cane to chew on. He say a little sweet just make you sweeter. So when yore lil girls get they sweet tooths give em some sugar cane, that not so bad."

We reached the street corner and there in the back of a parked pickup stood a man dressed in Sunday best, Bible in his left hand, preaching to a small crowd standing around the truck. In his right hand he was holding a large wooden cross with an equally large Bugs Bunny stuffed animal nailed to it. As he preached, he pounded the cross up and down in the pickup bed, the sound of the wood on steel putting emphasis on his sermon. We stopped and listened, standing a distance from the crowd.

"Buzz! Who and what in the hell is this all about?"

"That old Amos Heide. He call hisself a preacher but he aint. What he doin as to religion is as useless as teats on a boar pig. He need to tell the truth and shame the devil. He nuttier than a squirrel turd. He do this every Easter and Christmas. He trying to get parents and kids to repent the commercialism a the holidays. My daddy told me a guilty dog barks the loudest and the sun don't shine on the same dog's tail all the time. Same true with Amos Heide out here on the street scaring young'uns. If you don't mind, James, I'd just as soon like to go on to the diner. I can't abide this."

We settled in a corner booth. The waitress brought menus. Buzz declined the menu and asked for whatever vegetables they had, cornbread and sweet tea. I ordered the same.

"I don't eat animals a no kind. They God's creatures too. Cept maybe not a snake. I think God put them with us to make us afraid. A snake be a trickster. They trick us to disobey what God tell us. I heard some peoples eat snakes but Lord knows I would not touch one."

Our orders arrived and I picked up my fork, then realized Buzz had lowered his head, his lips moving in silent prayer. I waited till he said amen.

"Buzz? That's a strange name. A nickname maybe?"

"That what the town folk call me. Have since I was a lil kid. Most folks round here would tell you I was dropped on my head when I a baby, meaning they think I lacking brains and crazy as old Amos Heide out there on the street. My daddy made sure me, my brothers and sisters got as much schoolin as we could. I was never tuned in to the same things as the town folk was and to them that made me different but it don't make me feeble minded."

"What do you mean by tuned in to the same things they were?"

"When I was a kid my daddy brought home a old transistor radio with ear plugs he found in the garbage and give to me. Even with batteries it wouldn't pick up no stations, but the more I listen, the more I hear. I hear beautiful gospel music and sometime the Lord talkin to me. They used to be a hardware store down the street a ways and they pay me to sweep the floor. When I finish I go outside and listen to my radio. Peoples would stop and say what you listening to and I hold out the ear plug but they don't hear nothing but buzzin. That when they give me the name Buzz. I still got that radio. You call me Buzz if you want. I done got used to it."

"What is your real name?"

"Real name's Asaph. Asaph Pryde."

"That's about as unusual as Buzz."

"It a biblical name. I don't remember much about my mama other than her name, Vashti. I was the last a ten children. She took to the ground when I was about five year old. I got a old faded picture a me sittin on her knee at home. She was a small, good lookin, and Daddy said, a religious woman. Daddy said she carry the religion in the family and he carry the spiritual. Vashti give all us children the blessin of biblical names. Daddy say when I born she take one look at me and say this is Asaph. He gonna be doin somethin really important one a these days."

"What does your name mean?"

"It mean the gatherer, the collector."

"Would you like some coffee? If you have time I'd like to know more about your daddy and the rest of your family."

"You reporter fellows shore do have lot a questions." He checked the watches along his right arm, seemed satisfied and said, "I take some coffee, I been out of it at home and been missing a good cup."

I ordered coffee and told the waitress to keep it coming. Buzz seemed comfortable and ready to share more of his life story.

"My daddy called Nebo. He was a contrary man. One day he speak and sing the gospel and next day he get drunk, fiddle, sing and dance till the drink take his legs. That didn't stop him. He'd lay flat on his back too drunk to stand and fiddle through the night. He couldn't keep a job. He made fiddles out a skinny cedar trees he cut down, carving them by hand, glued them together with water and egg whites and added nylon strings. He walked the woods lookin for dead dogwood trees and made crosses held together with twine. He'd take all that downtown in a big basket, sit on the street corner and play and sing to draw a crowd. He sold a few fiddles and crosses but mostly to folks passing through town on their way somewheres else.

"Daddy raised all ten of us young'uns. He would take us on picnics to the graveyard where the black folk was buried. He'd bring his fiddle, play, dance and sing to the dead. He call it celebrating they resting place. He say, 'What the dead want with flowers and tombstones? They want music. Everybody like music, song and dance. I sing to they souls and remind them a the peace they found. The same peace I know I find one day.' Then he say 'When I go I want you children to do the same for me. Don't come bringin flowers or tears. Come and raise your voices in song and dance. The good Lord knows I will love that!'

"Your daddy sounds like quite a character."

"Yessir, that he was. Peoples would see us in the graveyard eatin our picnic as Daddy fiddled, danced and sang and they'd yell, 'Crazy old Nebo, get outta that graveyard and take yore poor young'uns with you. You aint never had much sense and even less after Vashti passed and left you to raise all them young'uns. Get outta there! Take them young'uns home! You walk and talk with the dead more than you do with live folks.' Daddy never paid em no mind. Just went on with his celebrating."

"You mentioned you were one of ten children. Are your brothers and sisters still living in this area?"

"I got one brother livin. Last I knew he was up in Philadelphia with a wife and half a dozen kids and workin as a mechanic. The rest a my brothers and sisters never left this mountain. Three brothers killed in car wrecks out there on Death Road. One drank hisself to death. One sister died in childbirth. Another a overdose a drugs. And the last two a my sisters were beat to death by they own husbands. My mama had the right idea givin us all biblical names but I guess what you try to sow in yore garden don't always thrive. I'm the only one left up here on the mountain."

He fell silent, a look of pain on his face. He raised his right arm and focused on the watch nearest his wrist, then quickly rose from his seat.

"I preciate the food and coffee but I gots to go. Enjoyed talkin with you. I be seein you soon."

He was gone before I got the bill paid and reached my car. The minute I got into the driver's seat I got a text from the office. Three-car accident north, mile marker 5 on Death Road. I arrived at the scene and there he was, just like every other time, leaning against the Olds.

That night I told Sarah about meeting Buzz for lunch. "I honestly don't know what to think of the old man. One minute he's sharing colorful memories of his family and childhood and the next talking about hearing gospel music and the Lord talking to him through the ear plugs of an old transistor radio that doesn't pick up any stations."

"James, the South is full of colorful, eccentric characters."

"That's just it, Sarah. I don't think he is eccentric. I think he means or at least believes everything he told me today. I've got to try and see him again. I have to know why he's always out there on Death Road at every accident, and more to the point, how did he know about the three-car wreck today even before I got the text from the office? That kind of creeped me out."

"Well, good luck, honey. It's good to hear you found a challenge here in the boring old South."

Six weeks passed and there were no accidents on Death Road. A group of people living along the offshoot dirt roads that led into it had gone to the city council with petitions demanding that stop signs be posted where the roads met. Don't get me wrong, I was relieved that the wrecks and deaths had stopped but at the same time could have kicked myself for not getting a phone number or address to reach Buzz. Within another four weeks the stop signs were shot up beyond readable and some even sawed off at the base or run over deliberately. The same people who filed the petitions resigned themselves to driving miles out of their way to get into town, avoiding Death Road. But there were still those who didn't care and tempted fate. The wrecks began once more, indiscriminate of age, race, day or night. Buzz was right there at the first scene.

"Buzz! It's good to see you again. Well, I mean not under these circumstances. You left the diner so quickly I didn't get a chance to get your phone number or find out where you lived."

"Yessir, I had hopes them stop signs would put a end to it, but didn't. It shore make the Lord and me more work. I aint got no phone but I live right up on the top a the mountain. Go right up that dirt road over there and keep goin till the road runs out. That where I live."

"I want to hear more about you and your family. Is there a good time for me to visit?"

"You come anytime. When I aint here, I home. I gots to go. About time to start cookin. I be seein you soon."

For the next four days torrential rains stalled over the mountain, refusing to move on, rutting and washing away dirt roads. I waited for a week before attempting the drive to the top of the mountain to see Buzz. The road was worse than I feared, water standing knee deep in the low places and what remained of the road consisted of random ruts. I drove up slowly, weaving from one high spot to the next. It took twenty minutes of this tedium before I reached the clearing atop the mountain. Buzz's car was parked beneath a big oak at the edge of the woods. I parked alongside the Olds and called out to Buzz. No answer.

In the distance I could see the remains of an old homestead. To the left among waist-high weeds stood a chimney and the wall it was anchored to. Opposite it, yards away there was a barn, swayback and leaning, part of the roof missing. There was no house that I could see and it struck me that Buzz might live in his car.

"James. I here!" Buzz emerged from the woods, carrying an armful of broken limbs and smiling.

"Hey, Buzz. Let me help you with that."

"Nossir. No need, I got it."

"I'm sorry I'm just now getting by to see you. I was worried about the roads with all the rain."

"Yessir. The Lord shore did send us some water."

"Is your house nearby?"

"Yessir, it right back behind the barn."

We walked in silence. There was such a stillness on the mountain, no wind, no insects, no sight or sound of birds or animals. We rounded the back corner of the barn where there was a path leading to a grove of trees in the distance. It was lined with rocks that ranged from pebble size to some so large I couldn't imagine how Buzz could have moved and placed them there. The tiny pebbles had little crosses painted on them. The medium size rocks painted with crosses and arrows pointing down the path toward the grove of trees. The large were painted with scripture. As we walked I read:

"I am the resurrection and the life. The one who believes in me will live, even though they die."

"For to me, to live is Christ and to die is gain."

"If we live, we live to the Lord and if we die, we die to the Lord. So, whether we live or die we belong to the Lord."

"He will wipe away every tear from their eyes and death shall be no more. Neither shall there be mourning, nor crying, nor pain anymore for the former things have passed away."

"I have fought the good fight, I have finished the race, I have kept the faith."

"Yes, we are of good courage and we would rather be away from the body and at home with the Lord."

We stopped in front of the last large rock before reaching the grove.

"Buzz, this is pretty cool. Are you a folk artist?"

"Don't know what that is so I reckon I aint."

I looked down reading the scripture:

"Let the little children come to me and do not hinder them for the Kingdom of heaven belongs to such as these."

"If not as an artistic statement, why would you put these along the path?"

"See them crosses and arrows back there? That show em the way. And them words from the Bible help get em ready for heaven. That one you just read is my favorite cause the lil children have the hardest time cause they not understand and they parents don't want em to go. My house is in that grove. I got us some coffee hoping you visit. Come on, I make us a cup."

We entered the grove, and a few yards in, the trees opened to another clearing. In the center was a Sunbeam bread truck, the tires missing, mounted on cinder blocks. It had to have been from the 50s. Little Miss Sunbeam, blond curls framing her face, looking down from the side of the truck with one blue eye. The other missing, replaced by a large spot of rust.

Innocent and poised, forever taking a bite out of a piece of buttered white bread. The slogan above her head, *Reach for Sunbeam! ENERGY-PACKED!* Under Miss Sunbeam the truck was lined and stacked head high with crosses of all sizes, the artificial flowers attached to them faded by the sun. I realized they were roadside crosses, many I recognized that were placed at accident scenes along Death Road and disappeared shortly after. An eighteen-foot four-by-four utility pole and meter leaned dangerously inward toward the truck, anchored by nothing but mud and rocks after the rain. A deep cast iron pot sat a few feet in front of the truck surrounded by ashes, bits of charred wood and odd shaped tree stumps.

I was beginning to feel uneasy, out in the middle of nowhere; no one knew where I was. My mind kept pulling back what Buzz had said a few minutes earlier, "That show em the way. Them words get em ready for heaven." What had I gotten myself into? An eccentric? A religious nut? A serial killer? Was I standing in his killing field? I could have turned and run but I was in, hooked, curious and fascinated.

Buzz opened the double doors at the back of the truck, reached up and pulled a chain. A yellowed light bulb flared to life, casting odd shadows. There was a hot plate sitting on top of stacked orange crates, the bottom crate on its side, filled with odd dishes, spoons, cups and one pot. Buzz turned on the hot plate, then pulled out the pot and two cups.

"I aint got no runnin water. Gotta go to the rain barrel."

While he went for water I looked about the room. There were more orange crates filled with clothes and blankets. One in the corner held a stack of newspapers, faded photographs and two Bibles, their covers worn and ragged. Buzz put the water on to boil, then shuffled through the stack of photographs.

"Here it be. This the picture I told you about. That my mama Vashti and that me on her knee. Was took in the old house out front that fell in now."

"Your mother was a pretty woman. So this is your family home site?"

"Yessir, my mama was pretty. Don't know how my daddy managed to find and hold onto her. But look at me. I was so ugly it hard to look straight on at me. Them Bibles over there belong to my mama Vashti and her mama Dakota. My daddy say Dakota mixed with some Indian blood. That and this land, about ten acres, all I got left. Course none a us ever had much. We was poor, bad poor. Poor folk like us had poor ways to survive. My sisters done ironing for the white folk in town. The youngest sister, Ruth, had to stand on a milk stool to reach the ironing board. My brothers cut wood and kindling off this ten acres and my job was to pull a little wagon full a wood that was made by my daddy out a junk yard parts. In town I go door to door with my wagon sellin the wood. Some days I do good and sell two loads a wood, then other days I be rocked and run out a folks' yards. One time we didn't have hardly no trees left up here to cut for wood to sell so my brothers, they sneak onto some white folks' property and cut the very wood I take the next day to they door and sell to them. I know it weren't right but we had to eat and that was the best way we knowed how. Coffee ready. Best we take it outside. It damp and stuffy in here after the rains."

The sun was high, and it felt good to be out of the confines of the truck. I started toward the stumps around the iron pot to sit and drink the coffee. Buzz began shouting, the first time I'd heard him raise his voice.

"No! No, James! Not there! That where I cook for em. I got some old lawn chairs out back. I bring us two to sit in!"

He set up the chairs and we sat for a while in silence, drinking our coffee.

"Buzz, who do you cook for?"

"The ones Death Road take."

"I don't understand."

"I didn't either at first. It took me a long time to figure out why my mama give me the name Asaph and say one day I be doin somethin important."

"Sorry, you told me once but I forgot what the meaning of your name is."

"Asaph be the gatherer, the collector. That what my mama knowed I be, soon as I was born."

"Buzz, I've got to tell you I'm confused about a lot of this. I have so many questions. Like how do you always know when there's been an accident? What's up with all the watches? And pardon me but you got to admit cooking for the dead does make you sound a little crazy. And all those roadside crosses over there, a lot of them I remember when they were put up on Death Road and disappeared days later. You know if they catch you taking them you could go to jail."

"Questions, that the reporter in you. I think it good we meet. Meant to be. That why I answer all yore questions, then you tell my story. Long as that road out there, they always be a need for a gatherer and a collector. Maybe you understand the need today or someday. I know when they gone be a accident cause the Lord tell me to get ready."

Buzz reached into his pocket and pulled out the transistor radio and ear plugs, holding them out to me. "The Lord tell me through my radio."

I took the radio from him, turned it on and put in the ear plugs. No stations, nothing but static and buzzing. "Buzz, I don't hear anything but static, maybe your batteries are corroded."

"Aint no batteries in it. Quit bothering with batteries. The gospel music and the Lord's words come anyway. Like I say to you one time, you got to keep on listening, then you hear. The Lord tell me to get these watches. Twenty-four, all set for ever hour a the day. Say it be two o'clock in the morning and that watch with that time be on my right arm and underneath it my skin get to itchin then I know it time to gather wood and get ready to cook cause soon my radio gone let me know another one comin. When I say I cook for the dead I don't mean real food, I cook for they spirit."

"What about the roadside crosses?"

"That a important part. You see, James, that really when I knew what I was meant to do. When peoples started puttin up them crosses where they loved ones died, I could see the dead they was honoring. They was still there, some standin, some sittin and some curled up beneath they cross. It trouble me and soon after the Lord told me I was to set them free, collect them and help them home. The Lord say they can see me like I see them and they would follow me. I bring em here and we sit by the fire, I sing gospel hymns and read scripture to em and give em they last meal. You see, when they look in that pot some see the dinner that was waitin for em at home when they was killed and some see they favorite meal. They favorite meal especially with the lil children. That calm em down and they not so afraid."

"But why take the roadside crosses and bring them back here?"

"Guess I tryin to make peoples see that them crosses hold they loved ones in a sorta limbo. Hold em in a place where they violent death happen and make em confused, scared and can't find they way to the Lord. That what the Lord need me for, to bring em back here and give em to him. Some peoples go and put another cross up after I take em down and some peoples get the feeling that they loved one is in the Lord's hands and they don't put up another cross. The crosses you see here is only a part of em. They hundreds more back behind this grove. They be more comin cause that road got a mind a its own, never shoulda been put there. I know this a lot to chew on but I hope you see the need a the job. I hope too that you aint thinking I feeble minded."

"Buzz, I'm not sure what I think. It's all pretty bizarre."

"You say one time you don't know much about the Bible, you smoke, drink and cuss. My daddy Nebo took the drink, he smoke a pipe and he cuss sometime but he was a spiritual man. I believe God know all you do but if you got his spirit in yore heart he understand. Takin a drink, smoke and say a cuss word don't make you a sinner like them that hurt and kill other peoples. Maybe one day you read the Bible. It a good book."

"That's true but I've covered news stories where men said God talked to them and told them in order to save their wives and children they must sacrifice them. Those stories made me think that religion and faith can be dangerous. It can make some people crazy enough to kill."

"That aint God talkin to them peoples, only the devil tell peoples to do such things. God do talk to peoples. He talk to em in different ways. Some peoples listen and some don't. It all about listening and believing. Too many peoples nowdays don't believe in nothing that they can't reach out and touch with they hand."

I left Buzz that day thinking he was eccentric and a religious nut. I told myself that he might not be dangerous now but could be in the future and decided to keep my distance. Sarah asked if there was a story in the old man. I told her it didn't pan out, nothing I could write that anyone would take seriously.

A year passed and I rarely thought of Buzz, but continued to see him along Death Road, the roadside crosses there one day and gone the next. I knew where they were, they were keeping company with hundreds of others and Little Miss Sunbeam. Buzz and I would wave or nod our heads, acknowledging one another at the accident scenes, but didn't speak.

Easter was a week away. Sarah said the girls were old enough for Easter baskets and an egg hunt. She bought matching frilly dresses, bonnets and shoes for Christie and Carrie and sent out invitations to all our friends and family and their children. She went all out, making decorations for the yard, cupcakes piled high with pale crayon colors of blue, pink and yellow icing. She had a list of things for me to pick up in town. Plastic Easter eggs, baskets, little bunny trinkets and lots of candy. This would be the year my girls got their sweet tooths. Amos Heide was there on the corner, holding his Bible, preaching the sin of Easter commercialism and pounding the wooden cross in the bed of the pickup. The Bugs Bunny stuffed animal was losing its stuffing, half of one ear missing and Bugs was barely clinging to the cross. I stood and listened but his sermon was the same litany as every Easter and Christmas, year after year.

Sarah was so excited. Lists of what to do and what to cook when were strewn about the kitchen counters. One minute she was sure she had everything she needed, the next she was making a new list and sending me back to town. All this and Easter still a week away. I was grateful to get back to the office Monday morning.

I was drinking my third cup of coffee, proofing the second page of the paper when the police scanner in our office sounded. An accident, south lane of Death Road. I knew the routine, grab notebook and camera. The phone rang, the editor picked it up, then waved to me.

"Wait, James!" He turned his back and spoke softly into the phone. "Yes. Uh-huh. I see." He turned to me, still holding the phone.

"James, I want to let another reporter get this one."

"Sure. Great! Does this mean I've been promoted?"

"Come into my office."

I followed, smiling, thinking it's about damn time they realized my potential. He closed the office door and we sat in silence. He picked up a pencil and chewed on the eraser, his head lowered. Then finally he raised his head, meeting my gaze.

"I can't let you cover this one. James, that was the police chief on the phone. I'm sorry, but that's your wife and kids out on Death Road."

"No! He's wrong! Sarah and the kids are home getting ready for an Easter Egg hunt."

"James, the chief knows you and your family. I don't think he's made a mistake."

"I got to go!"

I started toward the door and he caught my arm and held me. "James! James, they're gone!" I broke free, angry and shaking. I had to get to Death Road. It was a mistake, a mistake, a mistake. Buzz would be there, he'd know it wasn't my Sarah, Christie and Carrie. Two miles out of town I picked up my cell and dialed home. Ringing, ringing, then voice mail. "Sarah! Pick up the phone! I have to know you and the girls are home and safe!" I drove, clutching the cell, waiting for a call back.

The barricades were still in place. The chief ran to me, catching me by the shoulders before I reached them. The air was thick with the smell of pine, gasoline and motor oil.

"James, you need to go on back to town. Sarah and your babies' bodies have been taken to the hospital."

"You are a damn liar! Get out of my way!"

"James, Sarah's mama and daddy are on their way to the hospital. That's where you need to be. There are arrangements to be made."

"Arrangements? The arrangements are already made for the egg hunt, remember, Chief, you and your wife and kids are invited. Now let go of me, I've got to go down there."

"No reason for you to go down there, James. Now turn around, get in your car and go back to town. Or maybe it would be best if I drove you."

"You've made a mistake, Chief. I got to go down there and see Buzz. Buzz will know it's not so."

"Buzz? You are losing it, James. Come on and get in my car."

I broke free of his grip and ran past the barricade. Splintered pine logs lay across the road, a jackknifed logging truck filled both north and south lanes, its nose jammed into the rock ledges that banked Death Road. Wedged between its front grill and rock and beneath the front wheels was Sarah's Honda.

For the next three weeks days blurred in and out. The grief, people coming and going, offering condolences, the funeral, the burial and then the quiet. I took a leave of absence from work. Sarah's mama came to clear away the moldy cupcakes and decorations for the Easter egg hunt but I wouldn't let her touch any of it. She wanted to donate Sarah's, Christie's and Carrie's clothes to the church's closet for the needy and I threatened her, telling her to get out of my house. I was frozen in time; Easter Sunday was still a week away. In my mind I replayed the scene over and over. Each time it took longer, slowing down to frame by frame. The smell of pine, gasoline, motor oil, logging truck, Honda. Then it hit me. Buzz was not there that day.

I turned my police scanner on and waited. Nine-forty-five, accident on Death Road. I drove to the location, one fatality, but Buzz was not there. Every time the scanner went off, day or night, I rushed to Death Road but Buzz never showed. Then one night only yards from where the oil stains left by the logging truck that took Sarah and the girls there was another accident. That's when I saw the three crosses standing in the grass next to the rock ledge. There was a large white one and smaller white ones to the right and left of it, all covered in plastic artificial flowers of pastel Easter colors. I drove to Sarah's parents' home.

"Did you put those roadside crosses out on Death Road?"

"Yes, we did, James. In honor and memory of Sarah and the girls."

"You shouldn't have done that without asking me! I don't want them there!"

"We've called your house and you are never there so how could we get your permission? Besides, we are the parents and grandparents and have a right to put them there with or without your permission!"

"I want them gone! You don't understand! Those crosses hold them there!"

"What are you talking about, James?"

"The damn roadside crosses, that's what I'm talking about. Buzz told me! The crosses confuse and trap them there, unable to move on, go to heaven."

"James, we're worried about you. Think maybe you need to talk to someone. A grief counselor or a—"

"A shrink? Is that what you were about to say? Yeah, I need to talk to someone. I need to talk to Buzz. To hell with the both of you! I'll take care of the crosses!"

Halfway to see Buzz I changed my mind, turned around, stopped at the Quick Mart, picked up beer and cigarettes and went back to Death Road. Maybe Buzz was sick and hadn't been able to remove the crosses. I would wait for him. I never returned to work. For six months I stood along the roadside drinking beer and smoking, waiting for Buzz to come for the crosses. The chief passed by often, slowed his car and waved. He didn't stop or give me any hassle about drinking in public.

That's one good thing I can say about the South: they respect and leave a man with a broken, grieving heart be.

I drank and gazed at the crosses, hoping and wanting to see the same things Buzz had seen. I wanted to see my Sarah, Christie and Carrie, but didn't. As the months passed I realized I had to take the crosses to Buzz. I went home, packed a small bag and family photos and grabbed two sixpacks from the fridge. I took one last look at the Easter decorations, empty Easter baskets, cupcakes, untouched candy and the stack of bills on the kitchen table. None of it mattered now. Power and water had been cut off for a month and the bank was foreclosing on the house. There was nothing left. I locked the door and went to Death Road.

It took five beers for me to quiet my nerves, run across the two lane and pull the crosses from the ground. I drove to the top of the mountain, the road still almost impassible and now grown over with weeds and small sprouting pines. Buzz's car was not there. I called out but no answer, just that quiet stillness like the first time I'd been there. I walked to the back of the barn and the path lined with scripture rocks was still there. Through the grove of trees the Sunbeam truck, roadside crosses, cast iron pot and stumps remained among knee-high weeds.

I knocked on the truck and called out to Buzz again but there was only silence. I opened the back doors and fumbled for the pull chain, pulled it. The yellowed light bulb flared. There was nothing, nothing but empty orange crates.

Then I noticed that on top of the crate in the corner, where once there had been the family Bibles and faded photos of Buzz and his mama, lay a new red leather-bound Bible. I picked it up. On the top of the first page there was something written in childlike penmanship. My vision was blurred; seven beers since noon was catching up with me. I took it outside in the sunlight, closed my eyes for a moment, then opened them to regain focus. It helped enough to read the short message.

God do talk to peoples. He talk to em in different ways. It all about listening and believing. Maybe one day you read this Bible. It a good book.

A wave of nausea set in, Buzz was gone and not coming back. Why and where had he gone? He had to know about Sarah and my girls. That's what he told me he did, called by God to be the collector and help the victims of Death Road on to heaven. Nausea turned to anger and I threw the Bible. It landed among the weeds near the iron pot, and a feeling of shame flooded me. I picked it up, dusted it off and returned it to the orange crate in the truck. The sun was fading. I pulled one of the lawn chairs from behind the truck, went to my car, got the last five beers, drank and wept till fatigue and darkness lulled me to sleep.

The sun woke me. I stood up, my head pounding, throat dry, my eyes burning and feeling like golf balls. My body stiff, the nausea back and I was disoriented. There was little Miss Sunbeam smiling down at me and I called out to Buzz. Then I remembered the events of the day before and that Buzz was gone. I needed water and food to stop the stabbing pain in my temples. When we first moved to the mountain Sarah had made up an emergency kit, telling me to keep it in my trunk because you never knew about conditions on the mountain. Inside were paper goods, first aid kit, water, crackers and cans of Vienna sausage.

The first round of water and Vienna came right back up. The second stayed with me and I began to feel human. I left the grove and walked up and down the path reading the scripture rocks. Then I remembered the red Bible. Did I imagine it? It was still there on top of the orange crate. I looked up the words on the scripture rocks, then read more of the scriptures.

I read late into the night, falling asleep on the floor of the bread truck. Dream after dream came. Sarah smiling up from the hospital bed, me holding the twins bundled in pink blankets out to her. Christie letting go of the coffee table and taking her first steps. Carrie taking her first steps a week later. Sarah and I cheering both times like our girls had won an Olympic medal. Sarah at the stove icing cupcakes, Christie and Carrie modeling their new Easter dresses; then the dreams grew dark. Police scanner screaming, Death Road, the smell of pine, gasoline and motor oil, logging truck, Sarah's Honda and...

"Daddee. Daddee. Where are you, Daddee?"

I woke covered in sweat, trembling "I'm here girls! I'm here!" I wept, screamed out, "Damn you, Buzz! Where are you? I can't do this alone!"

Then I heard him, a slight whisper in my ear, his voice coming in and out between static. "It... in... the believing... Aint somethin... you can reach... out and touch...with your hand."

The next morning I began pulling weeds from the scripture path. In two days I cleared the path and all the weeds surrounding the truck. On the third day I collected wood and stacked it around the iron pot. The fourth day I got up early and waited for the time. The time of day I knew Sarah and the girls were lost on Death Road. A half hour before the time I started the fire and took their roadside crosses from the backseat of my car and placed them under Miss Sunbeam.

I sat on the stump nearest the fire recalling their favorite foods. Sarah, always health conscious, baked chicken and broccoli; Christie, macaroni and cheese; Carrie, pizza. I imagined it and added it all to the pot.

Time. Time. Time. I tend the fire, stir the pot, read the scriptures, believing, listening and waiting for the sound of their footsteps along the path.

X.

The Missives

Kilby Correctional Facility

Montgomery, Alabama August 10, 1980

Dear Archie,

I received a long letter from my aunt today. She caught me up on all the news back home. My cousin is expecting her second child. My brother remains well and has gone to work in the coal mines. Grandmamma and Granddaddy are doing good and still living at the farm. It was great to hear all is fine back home as Will and I rarely get to make the trip for visits.

In the last paragraph of the letter my aunt told me you were sent to prison for murdering Jeffrey. She said she knew little of the trial and could only tell me what she had heard through neighborhood gossip. I have read that paragraph over and over and still my mind will not let it be true. Jeffrey was among our closest friends and you Archie were his best friend! My aunt tells me she thinks you were sent to the Kilby Correctional Facility so I am writing you at this address. I hope what she has written me is only gossip and this letter to you comes back to me marked "Return to Sender/Not at this Address". Then I'll know you have not harmed Jeffrey and are not in prison and what she's heard is all lies.

Always,

Lilly

Birmingham, Alabama December 7, 1980

Hey Lilly

Yeah Im here. Ben here ninty days an thay got me on daly lokdown. Thay dont let no new prisners git leters or visters far tha firs thre munths. Thar werent much a trial. Thay jus haul me in thar an says gilty an nex mornin put me on a prisner bus ta Kilby. Ya kno I aint nevr had much scole. I staid ajet not wantin ta git in mor troble. Lilly I aint no murderer. But yeah I did kil Jeffrey. It jus happin an that all thay is.

Im glad ya sen me a leter. Thay dont treet me bad here an tha food is good but I shore do git lonly. Mos a all I mis bein outdors comin an goin lik I pleas.

I hope ma June Bug gits ta com se me soon. Got a leter fom her to an she says she wil be comin soon as she git herself a ride. She says she aint bringin Lil Archie cause she dont wont him ta se his dady loked up. I understan but shore would lik ta se ma lil boy.

I got ta go now. Thay turn off tha lites in a few minits an I got ta giv ma pinsel bac ta tha gard. Pleas sen me a nother leter.

Say hello fom Archie ta Will an yore swet lil gurls.

Yore friend

Archie

Kilby Correctional Facility

Montgomery, Alabama December 14, 1980

Dear Archie,

God help you! I have so many questions. How did this happen? Over the years our families have had such good times together. And in all those years I have never seen you angry or even raise your voice or hand to anyone. It just doesn't seem possible that you could ever harm much less kill Jeffrey.

How are June and Little Archie? Has June been able to visit you? Is there anything we can do to help her? Is there anything that you need we could send you? I am glad they are treating you well. How long will you be in prison? Please stay in touch and try to remember the good days.

We remain your friend,

Lilly

Birmingham, Alabama December 21, 1980

Lilly

God dont need ta wast non a his time halpin a dum sumbitch lik me. I was stewpid an done it ta ma self. I hope he halps ma June Bug an Lil Archie. I aint nevr ben a angre man an I werent angre at Jeffrey wen it happin. It jus happin. Im glad yall werent here ta se wha happin ta Jeffrey. Ya kno he drunk a lot a whisky an then he got ta puttin stuf up his nos an in his arm. He change. It made em *bad* crasie.

June Bug com ta see me one time. Thay hav a outdors walkin place an we got ta viset. She brung me cigarets an thay let me smok outdors. She says Lil Archie dont kno why I dont com hom. I mis em an wish I was thar ta tak em ta tha crick.

She may not git ta com no mor far visets cause she had ta go liv wit her mama up in tenesee. Jeffreys famlie was so mad thay was threatin ta hurt her an ma lil boy. Som of em drov by tha traylor one nite an shot threw tha winders whil June Bug an Lil Archie was inside. She was so fraid nex mornin she gits a ride ta town an tak tha bus ta her mamas. She call me this week an says to days after she lef sombody burn down tha traylor an word is that non a us can ever com bac thar ta liv or thay kil us. I dont feel bad bout wha I done ta Jeffrey I feel bad bout wha I done ta ma on famlie.

Im glad June Bug an Lil Archie ar wit her mama. She wil tak care of em an thay wont hav ta be fraid all tha time. Pleas dont say nuthin ta yore aunt or no body bout June Bug an Lil Archie goin ta tenesee. I wouldnt put nuthin pas Jeffreys famlie an fraid sinc thay cant git ta me theyd try an find them.

Thay say I wil nevr git out a prisen an nevr is a long time. I hope I dont go crasie lik Jeffrey. I mis watchin tha sun com up an go down. But mos a all I stay lonly.

Cristmas wil be here in a day or so an if I was hom I would hav alreadie cut a ceder tree an hav it up far Santie ta com se Lil Archie. I mis at to.

Thay aint nuthin I need ya ta sen but mor leters. Im reminberin tha good times we all had. Lik how all us would go out ta tha woods ta pic drie wild weeds an pine cones ta put on tha Cristmas trees. Thak ya far bein ma friend.

Archie

Kilby Correctional Facility

Montgomery, Alabama January 10, 1981

Dear Archie,

We went home for Christmas and I am just now getting to write back to you. Santa Claus was good to our girls this year. They got everything on their wish list. I cannot imagine how hard it must have been for you to not be home with your family this year for Christmas. How did you pass the time? Did they give you a good Christmas dinner?

My family wanted to know if I had been in contact with you. I told them we were writing each other. They didn't think it was a good idea for me to be writing you. Said Jeffrey's family was crazy and out to get you, your family and your friends. They said you must be crazy too to have killed him.

My aunt asked if you had told me why you killed Jeffrey and I told her no. She said I probably never really knew the real Archie, the Archie who was capable of murder and I should be afraid of you. She knew about the trailer burning and June and Little Archie leaving but no one knows where they went. I did as you asked and didn't say anything about them living with her mama.

My aunt also knew the whole story of what happened between you and Jeffrey that night. She told me you were down by the deep part of the lake, the two of you sitting in his car. Said you two must have gotten into a fight and you shot Jeffrey six times, then put him in the trunk of his own car and pushed it into the lake. She said the most disturbing part to her was that you were wearing Jeffrey's boots when they arrested you. Said there was something wrong with any man that would do that to a best friend and again she warned me against staying in touch with you.

Archie, I am not afraid of you and will continue to write and support you but I have to ask you once again. How did this happen? My aunt also said they found an empty bottle of whiskey and at least a dozen beer cans in Jeffrey's car when they pulled it from the lake. Were you both drinking heavily that night? Is that why there was a fight that went wrong? I tend to believe only a little of what my aunt tells me. So will you please tell me what really happened? It will stay between me and you, my friend.

Devotedly,

Lilly

Birmingham, Alabama January 20, 1981

Lilly

Thay giv us a ham dinner wit swet taters green beans an a roll. It wouldnt nuthin lik hom cookin. June Bug call me on cristmas day and she say thay didnt hav no ceder tree but her mama got presets far ma lil boy. I spended cristmas reminberin tha good times lik ya said. I reminbered tha las cristmas we all had a git togather. Ya an June Bug makin cornbred peling taters an snapin beans. Me an Will smokin tha turky an Lil Archie an yore gurls runnin an playin in tha yard. That was a good cristmas wit good hom cookin.

Me an June Bug is glad we got ya as friends. Yall nice folks. Ya husbon is a good dady an he work hard. He a yanke but he fit in wit all us. We lik hearin stoies bout wen ya liv up noth an com bak hom ta liv lik a souther. Ya ar a good mama. We alays lik comin to se yall. Ya alays had good musice playin an ya hous smeld lik wood smok an ya smeld lik rain. I mis tha smeld a rain. Mos time I dont kno if it rainin or tha sun shinin.

Ya reminber all us gettin in tha picup an goin ta tha crick far pinics. Lil Archie an yore gurls lik eatin penut buter sanwich an puttin thar feet in tha water. Ya reminber me gettin uner tha brige ta warsh off ma legs an yore lil gurl throwed a big rock off tha brige an hit me on tha top a ma hed. Dam neer kocked me out. Ya was gonna a wip er an I says no. Shes jus playin an didnt meen me no harm.

I ben thinkin bout June Bug havin ma lil boy. Shes a lil woman an had a hard time. Wen Lil Archie com out hes tha ugglist lil thang I ever seen. June Bugs mama says he look jus lik me an I laft. Ever yare he growed he look mor lik me. Pore lil thang wis he got his mamas look.

I ben thinkin bout Jeffrey to. I knoed em all ma life. He was thar wen me an June Bug marrie an was thar wen Lil Archie was born. We had meny a good time. I had a stop thinkin bout Jeffrey an them days.

Lilly I wont to com hom so *bad*. I wont ta *be* a kid agin. I wont ta gro up agin an all this go away an nevr happin.

Archie

Kilby Correctional Facility

Montgomery, Alabama February 25, 1981

Dear Archie,

I have waited to reply to your last letter hoping you would write again answering my questions.

It is great that you are remembering the good times. I have the same good memories. I also know how hard it has to be for you locked away indoors all the time. If June had let you, you would have eaten, bathed and slept outdoors.

It may be hard to think about Jeffrey right now but you have to understand that as your friend I need to know the truth about what happened. And as your friend I think you owe me that.

There are times when all of us want to be a kid again, grow up and change things that have happened in our lives. Truth is, it is not possible. That only happens in movies.

So once more I ask you these questions.

Were you and Jeffrey drinking and got into a fight?

Did you shoot Jeffrey six times?

Did you put him in the trunk of his car and push it into the lake?

Were you wearing Jeffrey's boots when they arrested you?

Always,

Lilly

Birmingham, Alabama April 16, 1981

Lilly

I had ta think a lon time fore I writ ya a leter. I reminber tha time I bought Jeffrey over ta ya hous lat one nite an yall was alreadie in bed. Yall got up an ya made us chese an cracters an put on musice. Jeffrey had ben drinkin whisky all day an nite. Roun midnite ya got tired an lay doun on tha flor nex ta tha recood plaer. Jeffrey was wantin ta danse an wen ya didnt git up he kiced ya. It made yore husbon mad an he was readie ta fite Jeffrey. I step in tha midle an stop ya husbon cause I knoed then that Jeffrey werent rite no mor an he woulda hurt yore husbon.

I alays feel bad bout it. I nevr shoulda bought em ta yore hous knoin wha he mite do drunk or mad. If ya reminber that was tha las time I ever bought him roun yall. I nevr fer get it an I nevr fergiv em far it. I went out ridin off an on wit

em but didnt hav em over ta ma hous no mor.
Didnt wont em roun ma June Bug an Lil Archie.

Tha day it happin Jeffrey pic me up erly mornin.
His grandady had died tha week afore an lef
Jeffrey a pockit ful a mony. He was alreadie
drankin whisky an wantin ta go gamling. We wnet
ta a bar at had dice throwin in a bac room.
Jeffrey losed a thouson dollors an was mad as
hell. We drov roun him drankin mor whisky an me
drankin beer. We wnet ta town ta a fancie shoe
stor an he git his self a par a cowboy boots. Thay
was som thin an cos em eigt hunred dollors. He
giv me is ol boots an we jus keep ridin an drankin.

It git late an we by mor whisky an beer an park
down at tha lake. We sat an talk an drank an he
count his mony. He had a big rol of it lef but he
gits ta thankin them dice at tha bar was riged an
he was wantin ta go bac an do som ass kickin. I
was tryin ta talk em out a it an wnet ta put ma
beer on the dasbord knoc it over an it spil on his
new boots. He cal me a clumsie sumbitch an afore
I new it he pull out his knif an cut me cros ma
ches. I try ta git out a tha car but he was stil
comin afer me. I had ma gun in ma pockit an

afore I new it I shoot em. An he stil kep comin an
I kep shootin.

I was stil pullin tha triger afer I new he was ded.
I was scaed Lilly. I didnt hav no chois. I kil em
but I aint no murderer. An yeah we was at tha
deep in a tha lake an I put em in tha trunk an
push tha car in. Ya dont hav ta be fraid a me
Lilly. Ya kno I wouldnt hurt none a yall. I hope ya
reminber me an kno me. If ya seen me now ya
mite not kno me. I git reel fat sittin up here in
tha pen. I sorrie ya famlie dont wont ya to sen
me no leters but pleas sen me leters.

Archie

Kilby Correctional Facility
Montgomery, Alabama April 26, 1981

Dear Archie,

How horrible! It sounds as if you didn't have a choice, that it was self-defense. Didn't your lawyer plead self-defense?

Thank you for telling me how it happened. I will continue to write and support you. But there is still the one last question you have not answered.

Why were you wearing Jeffrey's boots when you were arrested? My aunt thinks you took them as a trophy after killing Jeffrey.

Always,

Lilly

Birmingham, Alabama May 14, 1981

Lilly

Didnt hav no lawer. Couldnt pay one. A man stod up wit me but he didnt say much. This wek thay tel me thay gone put me on a nother prisner bus an tak me ta Holdman Prisen. A nother prisner tol me tha Holdman Prisen is in tha countrie wit woods an farms roun it. I dont gues I git ta se them woods an farms cause at prisner tol me ats whar thay tak ya ta kil ya. So I gues thay gone kil me. Funie how thangs go roun. Soner a later we all gotta die but I shore aint reedy jus yet. If thay let me hav leters ya wil hav ta sen ma leters ta Holdman.

I done tol ya wha happin at nite why I kil Jeffrey an ya stil wanna kno bout tha boots. I mak a deel wit ya. Ya alays lik dansin. One nite in yore kichin ya an me was dansin an ya tol me ya reel name werent Lilly but ya lik ta be cal Lilly. I wil tel ya bout tha boots in this leter if ya tel me ya reel name in yore nex leter.

I tak Jeffreys boots an was wearin em wen thay pic me up an tak me ta tha jail. Yore aunts wrong. It werent nuthin lik at. Them boots werent no trofy. Ya tak a ders anlers an a coons tale wen ya kil em far a trofy. Jeffrey mite a ben actin lik a wild anmal at nite but he was ma friend. Ma friend all ma life. I had ta kil em or he kil me. I fel reel bad bout wha I done an I jus wantin ta keep a lil a Jeffrey wit me. I dont thank Jeffrey woulda ben mad at me far takin his boots. We was lik brothars.

Thay aint tol me wen thay gone kil me wen I git ta Holdman. I reel tard an wis I knoed if I wil go ta heven. If I git in heven I wander if I be a kid agin lik I wis. I dont thank I wil writ no mor leters. I wil wate far yore leter wit tha anser ta ma questen.

I reminber a song fom tha musice ya alays play. It were one of ya favrites. I dont reminber who sung it but I reminber tha words.

Wen thay tak me ta kill me I wil be thankin of ya an sanging this song.

I liv on a big roun ball

I nevr do dreem I may fall

An even one day if I do

Well I jump up an smil bac at ya

I dont even kno whar we ar

Thay tel me we cirling a star

Well I tak thar word I dont kno

But I dizzy so it mus be so

I ridin a big roun ball

I nevr do dreem I may fall

An even tha hi mus lay low

But wen I do fall I wil be glad ta go

Yeah wen I do fall I wil be glad ta go

Holman Correctional Facility
Atmore, Alabama May 28, 1981

Dear Archie,
I will miss you, my friend.
My name is Jan.

Jan Fink

About the Author

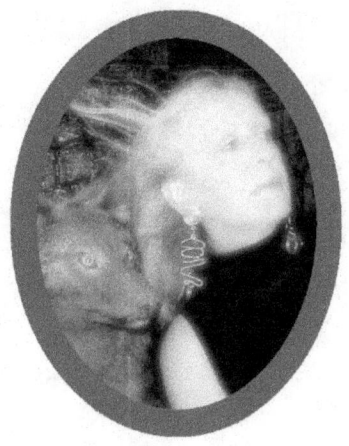

Jan Fink was born in Alabama and raised in the farmlands outside Tuscaloosa during the 1940's and '50s. She escaped rural life to New York in the late '60s, where she met her husband, Will. They currently live in Arab, Alabama where she is working on her first novel.

Jan has worked as a reporter, newspaper columnist and has been featured in Deep South Magazine's "Southern Voice." Jan's writing is influenced by the sometimes light and inevitably dark sides of Southern life.

www.ingramcontent.com/pod-product-compliance
Lightning Source LLC
Chambersburg PA
CBHW070446030726
47503CB00004B/922